How Far She Went

Winner of

How Far She Went

Stories by Mary Hood

The University of Georgia Press
Athens

© 1984 by Mary Hood
Published by the University of Georgia Press
Athens, Georgia 30602
All rights reserved

Set in Linotron 202 Baskerville

The paper in this book meets the guidelines for
permanence and durability of the Committee on
Production Guidelines for Book Longevity of the
Council on Library Resources.

Printed in the United States of America
88 87 86 85 84   5 4 3 2 1

Library of Congress Cataloging in Publication Data

Hood, Mary.
    How far she went.

    (The Flannery O'Connor award for short
fiction)
    Some of the stories first appeared in *The
Georgia Review.*
    Contents: Lonesome road blues—Solomon's
seal—A man among men—[etc.]
    I. Title. II. Series.
PS3558.O543H6 1984   813'.54   84-1375
ISBN 0-8203-0723-8 (alk. paper)

Acknowledgments

"A Country Girl," "Doing This, Saying That, to Applause," "Manly Conclusions," and "Inexorable Progress" first appeared in *The Georgia Review*.

"Lonesome Road Blues" first appeared in *The Ohio Review*.

"Inexorable Progress" was selected for inclusion in *The Best American Short Stories 1984* (New York: Houghton Mifflin Company, 1984).

For LITTLE VICTORIA,
big enough

. . . let us die in abstinence
Of one another, sigh gales, yet refuse
To speak the solving word which opens chaos . . .

Howard Nemerov,
"False Solomon's Seal"

Contents

Lonesome Road Blues

There hadn't been any rain and there wouldn't be any rain, so the water trucks came along and dampened the paths of the fairgrounds just before opening time. Under the shade of the oaks and hickories it was cool now, but the sun would persist until it and the wasps had drunk the gravel dry. Shirts would stick to damp backs and by noon there would be a darkening stain around men's hatbands. The flies would fatten at the food booths and settle drowsily on the sticky benches. No matter how hard the musicians hammered the dulcimers, it wouldn't drown out the locusts as they raged in the leaves overhead.

A solitary woman wandered from booth to booth, watching the craftsman maul white oak into shingles, examining the quilts and the corn sheller, studying the other lost country arts and machinery on display. Long before showtime, when the ticket line began to form, the woman took her place and stood, in all that paired-up, child-burdened crowd, single, unencumbered, serene. She rested her eyes on the blue-green mountains beyond and beyond the shimmering steel music hall inside its excluding fences.

She stood very straight, her spine purposeful more than righteous; she looked like a person who would do what was necessary, who had more than a nodding acquaintance with Duty. For all her quietness, her eyes were quick, as though the color and movement around her were a feast and she had been long starved. She had the pallor of the sickroom upon her; even so late in summer as this she was winter pale. There were hot crescents of sunburn on the tops of her shoulders where her sleeveless dress had left her vulnerable.

"One," she said, as she stepped up to the ticket seller. He pushed his hat back and looked at her, playing to the crowd. They had plenty of time, no hurry. He said, heartily, "Pretty little ol' gal like you might *arrive* alone but I bet you'll leave with a sweetheart. . . . bet you teach school, don't you? I always was the teacher's pet." He held her hand to count her change into it. "If you don't get lucky, you come on back by here this evening, I'll think of something," he teased. She pulled her hand free of his paw and pushed her way through the stile into the lobby. Somebody behind her testified, "Jim and Jesse's worth the price of admission theirselves," and another fan was saying doubtfully, "Everybody ought to come here at least once, anyway."

There was a line for the rest rooms too. She waited, as she had all her life, her turn. In the lavatory mirror she glanced at herself. Did she look like a schoolmarm? She *had* taught school years ago, before she married. Not having a comb with her, she smoothed her hair with her hands, then stepped back, yielding the mirror to two girls who with a shared satchel of cosmetics transformed themselves without embarrassment, silently, expertly. The blonde unbuttoned her blouse and rolled it, tying the tails above her navel. The other girl climbed up onto the sink itself to sit as she licked her contact lenses and put them in her eyes, then painted the lids with bright color, leaning close, within kissing distance of her own reflection. She worked fast, finished, and hopped down, turning her back on herself, looking over her bare shoulder, appraising her derriere. She had to stand on tiptoe to see. She rolled her shorts two turns at the waistband to bring them up even higher on her thighs. "How about now?" she asked her friend, and the other girl said, "Yeah," and they went out, leaving behind them a faint vanilla wake. "How many miles is it to Babylon?" an old lady murmured as the door closed. "When I was a girl, we didn't have to paint on our blushes." She was still holding forth when the solitary woman left to find her place in the auditorium. She chose a vantage toward the front, center. The hall had begun to fill.

The first few acts were local groups. One quartet wore identical white suits with lightning silver-sequinned down the sleeves and legs. They sang over their ruffles in close harmony and finished to strong applause and rebel yells. Then the Grape Arbor Pickers performed, dressed as though they had just come from the fields. The big bassman unbuttoned his chambray shirt and let it fall to his waist, like an apron tied on backwards. The wooden crucifix on his hairy bare chest gleamed, and the leather thong it hung from blackened with sweat.

A cheerful latecomer standing uncertainly in the aisle predicted to all those around, "Somebody's going to *faint*. Them fans doing no good atall."

There was an intermittent flicker of flashbulbs, like heat lightning. Applause like chicken frying. The curtains swept closed, and the emcee announced, "No need to leave, stay for the second show, stay all evening, buy supper on the grounds, plenty of good things to eat, be a lot cooler by then, more fine music to hear, stay and see if my mama raised me to lie to good people from all over, anyone from Texas? Texas! Glad to have you. How 'bout Mis'sippi? Yeah? And where? U-taw by the Great Salt Lake? Well, that was a long dry drive, wasn't it, folks . . ." He glanced over his shoulder, with a questioning look, seemed to be listening, then nodded. "About ready up here, folks, so welcome if you would, then, ladies and gentlemen, Mister Edmun Lovingood, one of the giants of Smoky Mountain banjo, remember last year? Tore up our pea patch, some fancy picker! Backed by (he consulted his paper) Neal and Bud, take it away, boys!"

The curtains opened. Neal introduced Bud and Bud introduced Neal and they turned and held out their beckoning arms for Lovingood, but he stood planted before his mike and would not be coaxed into the glare. "You could practice a hundred years and never be as good as him," Bud said. The applause acknowledged that to be true; they had all heard him play favorites; they hollered and stamped and slapped and clapped. "Yeah!" Neal cried, and Bud tapped his bow against his fiddle in tribute to the master. Lovingood raised his picking hand to his hat-brim in salute, in slow motion, patient in the generous uproar, the metal picks on his fingers sending out little reflections, like struck sparks. Now he dropped that hand back onto the strings and away they all raced to the end of "Whoa, Mule!" This was the real thing. Authentic, no electric instruments, no drums, no pop undertow dragging you from the fields toward the city, just clean, clear bluegrass, classic. The standing-room crowd moved a little forward, and a few devoted fans surged down to the foot of the stage itself to stand and gaze up. Bud and Neal, as good as they were, were all but swept away before the current of Lovingood's playing, incessant, driving, like a river in full spate. One after another the tunes poured forth:

"McCormick's Picnic"... "Train 45"... "John Hardy"... "Soldier's Joy"... "Dog River"... "Lonesome Road Blues"... "False-hearted Love"... In the middle of that one a lithe blonde in cutoffs dashed for the stage and tried to vault up; she was dragged away sobbing by her parents. Another young woman pressed forward, waiting till the song ended to hand up a note. Neal reached down to take it into custody. He had to lean way over to hear her special instructions. He stood and announced, lighthearted, accustomed, "Got a message here for Mr. Edmun Lovingood himself, a message for Ed—"

Someone in the hall yelled, "What does it say?"

Neal shook his head, grinning. "No, she don't want *me* to read it, it's for Edmun." He glanced down at the girl's uptilted face with its rouged cheeks. "A private personal message." She nodded and said something. "An emergency," Neal translated into the mike for everyone's ears. She raised both hands and nixed that. "*Not* an emergency," he clarified. He passed the note along to Bud, who raised it to his nose and sniffed, eyebrows way high, as he hollered, "Whoooeee!" and stepped on down to Lovingood, who took the paper in his left hand, just stood where he was planted for the duration with that patient impassivity. He took the note in his two fingers and without glancing at it deposited it in his vest pocket. Without visible cue, without missing a beat, away they all went on "Cumberland Gap." The brightly painted young lady returned to her seat, getting a good hand from the audience, as though she had played a quick break with grace and style. Lovingood never looked down at her, just kept his eyes on the back of the hall and played on, his face masked in inert sadness, his whole figure without elegance, unkempt, his boots run-down, his pants too wide at the cuff for fashion, shiny, baggy-kneed from hard travel, his vest unbuttoned, his collar tight under his chin, a black tie knotted hard against his Adam's apple, never mind what kind of weather it was. As though he didn't give a damn. That was it. And even without giving a damn he was more interesting than all the others, a genius, the solitary woman thought. She sat with both hands in her lap, a good-girl pose, brought up on the lifetime pleas of mother and aunts to be a lady, be a lady if it kills you. She pressed her hot eyes shut, tight enough to see fireworks, and when she opened them, there he still stood, like a sleepwalker on the stage, playing in a dream, his hands knowing what to do, his fingers wise as they danced on the strings. His hands might have been enchanted. She leaned a little forward, watching. This was what she had come for.

Her pulse picked up the tempo of "Orange Blossom Special." She smiled at the contempt and alienation on Lovingood's face; it grew more pronounced as he dazzled them with his version of the general favorite. Men jumped to their feet, waved their caps, whistled. She thought the gusts of admiration would surely topple him; he swayed back, exhausted, as he finished the song. He looked very tired. He looked as though he might have driven all night to make this engagement, arriving without time to spare for a shower, a nap, a decent meal. He looked (and this is what hurt her) as though his weariness were habitual.

Bud announced that after their show there would be tapes and albums on sale in the parking lot. "Just come on around there and talk to us, you're why we do it, maybe Edmun'll give you his autograph, he knows 'X,' we've been teaching him, just kidding, Ed, but folks come on out and meet us, we're here to please you, we're just folks and you're just folks, and you're why

we do it, you make it all worthwhile . . ." Then, in
another of those cueless miracles of spontaneity, they
all began "Darlin' Corey" at the same instant. During
the chorus Lovingood dropped out for a moment,
raised his hat with his right hand, and passed his left
arm in its damp sleeve over his face. He didn't glisten
like the others; he wore no makeup at all. Had no
vanity at all, it seemed, as though it were pawned
somewhere miles back or lost with luggage, and now all
that counted was playing to the end of the road. En-
durance, that was what he had.

"Pretty Polly" next, then "Earl's Breakdown," then
"McKinley's White House Blues," and finally, "Dixie,"
and while the crowd still roared on its feet the curtains
closed. When they opened again, only Bud and Neal
were left onstage, Lovingood had gone. Neal and Bud
swept their hats low in thanks. Lovingood did not come
back out though the audience raved the drapes open
once, twice more. Lovingood had done. No encores.
"Come back at seven for the evening show," Bud in-
vited. "And don't forget we'll be selling those albums
and tapes . . ." The curtains closed again, this time for
intermission.

There was a stir as the audience rearranged itself,
some leaving entirely, others hastening out to the con-
cession stand, others queuing up at the rest rooms.
Over the PA the emcee promised, "Jim and Jesse,
they'll be next, folks, and they've brought a surprise or
two with them! We're getting the red carpet rolled out
right now, so stay tuned."

But the woman had come to see Lovingood, not Jim
and Jesse. She went out the rear doors into the lobby.
The way was clogged by the milling crowd as they
bought refreshments or souvenirs. She turned aside,
impatient, and went out the nearest door. The whole

building opened like a warehouse, the steel walls
rolling up on tracks like garage doors. The door she
had chosen led to a patio; there was no way down to
the ground, no steps, just a drop of about five feet to
the bare red clay below. She turned back into the hall
with its stale summery smell of tired and dirty children,
damp babies, cheap food, tobacco, oniony sweat. She
crossed the hall and went out the doors on the opposite
side, walking with such purpose she attracted a following, who suspected she knew something that they
didn't; greed and self-interest woke. Some hastened
past her, to get there first, wherever it was. Dead end,
that was where. She had come up to a fenced-off area,
no way past, though she could see the parking lot,
could see where she wanted to be through the chain-
link fence. Frustrated, she swung back; the crowd had
thinned now, and she left by the main doors, out
through the ticket stile, and down along the fence on
the graveled road leading around back. From the open
doors wafted the announcement: "Special surprise—
Lonzo and Oscar!" Screams and cheers and laughter as
the two clowns took the stage. The applause was like a
magnet, drawing all strays back into the hall. The parking lot was deserted. She made her way on alone, past
the motor homes and vans of the major stars. At the
far end of the lot, in the receding shade, a dusty station
wagon stood with its tailgate down. Lovingood stood by
it, talking with another man, whose confidential and
enthusiastic posture was that of a fan. The woman
dawdled, wishing the fan would have his say and go.
Go! she willed. She paused as a gust of sparrows settled
in the shadow of a car, pecking at browned cores,
broken French fries, bits of crust. The fan kept on
talking. Lovingood's face, in the shade of his hat-brim,
wore its same impassive expression, that patient, unin-

volved weariness as he replied, "Yeah" and "Maybe so," dredging up the answers from that deep grave where courtesy lay not quite dead. The fan aimed his camera, adjusted, clicked it. Now he noticed the woman and held out the camera to her, saying, "Just one of us together, thanks," showing her what to push, how to frame. She did what he told her, then handed the camera back. He dropped it in his shirt pocket, picking up his record album and finally, finally going.

But he remembered something and turned back. "No singing on this one, is there?" He studied the jacket for some clue. "I like the instrumentals, what I do." Lovingood stood there shaking his head slowly, without conviction; he didn't remember. The woman looked at the album and said, absolutely certain, firm, proprietary, "No singing." She surprised herself. She smiled. The fan took her word for it and wandered off across the wasteland toward the music hall. He tapped the album against his lean thigh. The sunlight flashed from the cellophane cover like a mirror. Lovingood blinked and turned away, began fitting the other records into the crate, out of the sun. Before he locked up he turned to her. "Something?"

"I bought them all last year," she said. She noticed the old quilt and dingy pillow. Was that where he slept? While the others drove?

He locked the crate and shoved it into the car, laying the quilt over it for insulation.

"I guess you wouldn't remember me," she said. "Just one of your many fans."

Up close he looked older than onstage; the blonde hair and mustache were shot through with silver. There were olive smudges under his eyes, hollows in his cheeks, vertical deeps she could fill with her finger if she dared to reach up and lay it there.

"They're killing you" was how she saw it, jealous, her ardent brown eyes taking him in.

"Wha' do you say?" His veiled gaze traveled past her and prowled on the green mountains beyond.

"A shower," she was saying, offering. "A clean bed. Clean sheets cool and sweet and line-dried in the sun. Quiet and peace. No traffic, no motion, no music, not even your own, just stillness . . . silence . . . sleep . . ." She told it in her low, lulling voice, one pleasure at a time. "Rest in a quiet room, a blue and green and white room like snow and sky and moss. Deep shade and a slow fan turning this way and that till you fall asleep in the cool. And on toward evening, waking to the sparrows chipping in the eaves, a thrush singing far off. Someone laying silver on a clean cloth, ice tapping against a pitcher, shining plates . . ." He gave a little start, like a man who has dozed off and waked on the same breath.

"Been a long time since the last time," he said. He drooped now on the tailgate, looking balefully around the lot at the glittering cars, at the motor homes, at the custom vans. The tar and dust and diesel and gasoline blended into a miserable musk against which (or for some reason) she held her breath. Jim and Jesse in a cloud of musicians, all shining in sunny yellow suits, hastened across the shadeless strip from their air-conditioned bus into the hall by the backstage door. Lovingood watched them drowsily, as a lion at the zoo watches school children.

"You're as good as they are," she said.

He rubbed his eyes. "It don't differ," he said. What impression could he have of her as she stood there, pale as a sketch, unremarkable? She had so much she wanted to say! The heel of his boot had been nailed back on crooked; it left a ledge for his other foot. He settled and drew out his tobacco and rolled a cigarette, lit up, inhaled all the way past his ankles, and let the smoke dribble out around his next question. "Wha' do you say?" Meaning anything, meaning it's your turn, meaning what next?

"I saw you here last year," she said. "You were wonderful. I think you were the best, no really! I was going to tell you later, after the show, but you looked so tired. I have all your records, I bought them all, an armload, and I wanted to ask you to come to supper with me, I live just down the road, but I said, 'No, I have no claim, someone else will surely . . .' Wishing it was so for *your* sake," she tried to assure him now, with her face turned full on him, then away again, her eyes restless as she read her thoughts from that mental page she had been composing all year. "Wishing . . ." But it was no good, she had lost her place. She lifted her hand to her forehead, pushed her hair back, hoping he would say *something,* but of course not telling him that. He just sat there smoking the cigarette down to his fingers, getting his money's worth out of the smoke. She sat beside him on the tailgate, smoothing her skirt under her, swinging her pale feet in their new sandals back and forth.

"I want you to have a friend!" she cried so softly not even the sparrow flying up to glean the bug-spattered grill of the truck parked next to them could have heard her.

But Lovingood heard her. The message passed through the cracks in his crust and into the quick, stinging, reminding him he was alive. He glanced at her profile, cool and pale and intense, but she wouldn't turn and look at him. She kept her head ducked, staring at her toes as she swung her feet, a wallflower on a hard bench at dance school.

"Hell yeah," he decided, spitting a bit of tobacco from the tip of his tongue, then with thumb and fore-finger brushing back his mustache so his teeth gleamed in the clearing. A bit of gold shone as he grinned, not in front, but way back—something tucked away for a rainy day.

She let out a slow breath that could have extin-guished forty candles on a cake. She gave a little jump down to earth. He locked up the tailgate and followed her.

"Your friends?" she wondered, looking back, looking around. There was no one in sight, not Neal, not Bud, not another fan. He looked too, but without much in-terest, then again that gesture—the lifted hat, the pass-ing of the sleeve over his features. She saw how his hair was thinning at the back.

"We're all free, white, and over twenty-one," he said. "They know to be back here at six-thirty, same as me."

They walked past the music hall to the parking ter-races. A hot breeze stirred the young maples, turning their leaves over, showing them silver to the sky. "Trees begging for rain," Lovingood said. "Where I come from that's what it signs," he added. "Here, I dunno." He looked at the sky, cloudless, and shook his head.

"Rain? It's forgotten how," she said. She couldn't re-member where she had parked. She stood trying to recall. There! One more terrace up. Lovingood took the shortcut, straight up the dusty red bank, grappling along with handholds of the sun-scorched grass which was fine and flaxen as a woman's hair. She clambered along beside him, lighter, less tired, and reached the graveled summit first, turned, holding her hands out to help him up. It was the first time they touched. They stood catching their breath after the rough climb.

His hand was very strong, broad-wristed; the only cal-
luses were on the nicotined fingertips, from bending
the banjo strings. She held his palm in her two hands
and read his fortune.

"So," she said, and turned to unlock the car. But they
had to stand a while longer under the grilling sun to let
the heat drain out of the car's interior. Finally she got
in, started the engine, and turned on the air-condi-
tioner. It blew hot, then cool. When he didn't get in
then, she glanced at him, anxious, but he wasn't looking like he had changed his mind, he was just standing
there with that solid patience that had no time and
took it all.

"Maybe now?" she suggested.

He did not seem like a man at bay, only in abeyance.
All the difference in the world, she knew that. There
was fire in him. Fire and wit. Hadn't she heard it in the
music? Seen it in his hands? Something God-given, a
burden, a grace, not something sequinned on a jacket
or topstitched on a boot. He was a master, not a star.
She trusted him for his plainness. With a sigh now, he
ducked his head (the hat stayed on, grazing the head-
liner) and got in. Immediately he slumped back against
the headrest and seemed to doze off. Habit? Suggest-
ing a vague hope that she wouldn't be a talker? She was
no talker; she didn't talk now for sure.

She headed them onto the asphalt main road to the
gates and out onto the state highway, north. They
rolled smoothly toward Carolina.

"What's it called?" he asked drowsily, from under
that sweat-foxed old hat. His eyes were barely open.

Life! Life! she wanted to cry in gratitude, but he
meant the mountain up ahead; she realized that in
time and said, "Joseph's Coat, for the way it looks in
October."

In another mile they turned off the main road onto a graveled lane and from there onto a narrower, scraped track. The dust-caked brambles, berry laden, were close enough to pick from the car windows. A mockingbird fluttered up, sailed to a stop on a fence post, and rested, wings outstretched, mouth agape.

Lovingood said, "He's thirsty."

She swerved the car onto the narrowest lane yet, found the ruts, and headed them for the homestretch, dodging the washtub-sized rock, easing them over the hump. "This is a county-maintained road," she said.

"I'm thirsty," he said, as though warning her.

"Well, I thought you would be," she said, smiling, pleased with herself. She had driven across the state line to buy it. "I got a bottle for you."

"Enough?" he wondered. He still seemed uneasy about it, but looked cheered, as though there might be room for hope, for probable good news.

She parked the car and set the footbrake before she held up her hands to show how big. "A half-gallon?" she wondered.

"I hope to God so," he said, laughing, and got out.

They were home. Here was the shade she had promised, and the quiet as well. She unlocked the door (how many keys she had! but she knew just which one it was, and her hands were steady) and followed him in. He went through the house, looking in all the rooms.

"Who else lives here?"

"No one else," she said quietly. If he had asked, she would have told him how her husband had died, lingering. The sickroom had leached her to the bone, had taught her the value of peace. She turned on the slow fan. Its drone worked on her nerves the way the whiskey did on his. He found it himself, lifted the whole bottle to his lips, then offered it to her. She did not drink, no; with a smile, she set the glasses back in the cabinet. "Is it all right?" She had been bewildered by all the labels, had stood in the store too shy to ask advice, had chosen at random.

"It flows downhill," he husked, giving it time to hit bottom, radiate out from his gut into the long bones, climb to the muscles in his neck, seep down into his leaden arms. She watched him, bright-eyed. "Jaysus," he groaned, realizing his weariness, so that his spirit matched his haggard face. He took the bottle with him into the bedroom, setting it on the floor in front of him, incentive to bend over, to pry off his boots. His socks were chafed into lace at heel and toe.

"Shall I start your shower? I'll turn on the shower," she decided, for it took a good while for the hot water to come from the tank on the back porch. She touched the razor, the soap, the towels she had laid out for him already. He was standing at the window watching a thrasher ferreting along under the hollies, stabbing at the black peat, gobbling, turning his hard little eye this way, that, stealing on. She touched his arm and said, "Whenever," and went out, leaving him to his own restorations.

In the kitchen she set the cut-up hen to soak in buttermilk. The beans were already snapped. The corn was still to be shucked and pared. She heard the shower on and on, or rather not the shower but the clank and tap of the hot-water pipes under the floor where she stood working.

She thought perhaps he should be the one to say which pie—berry or peach. She went to ask. Floured hands up, she rapped on his door, then elbowed it open. He had not even begun to bathe. He lay on the bed where he had fallen, exhausted, trying to extricate his wrist from his sleeve. The rest of the shirt lay on the floor by his boots. She turned off the water, then came back and gingerly unbuttoned the cuff and pulled the shirt free, the rest of the way, claiming it for the laundry. He rolled over on his side and groaned, but never woke. His hat hung on the whiskey bottle like a natural peg, as if he had tossed it—a lucky shot. The level in the bottle was down a good two inches.

She went out and closed the door.

He slept till after five o'clock. She was frying the last of the chicken when she heard the hot-water pipes clang, and she knew he was up. She stepped out onto the back porch to check his shirt; it was as white as she could get it, and nearly dry at the seams. She brought it in and laid it on the chair back, humming. She gave a moment's attention to the food on the stove, then stepped into the dining room to admire the pies. She had made both, let him choose if he could. They stood butter-crusted and plump on their trivets. At the sound of the bedroom door opening, she hurried back into the kitchen, neutral ground.

Then there he was, standing by her sink, his polished boots (if he noticed their buffed shine, he never said so) in one hand, the liquor in the other. She expected him, but it still amazed and pleased her so she had to look quick, then look away. Cooking and happiness had put some color into her face and steam had frizzed the fine hair, softening her forehead; she felt young. She stirred their supper in seven pans, gave a glance at the contents of the oven. He sat and pulled the boots on over a pair of her husband's socks she had laid out, then stood and drew on the clean shirt, buttoning, tucking it in quickly, like a man used to dressing without looking glass or leisure.

"I was going to iron it!" she protested. "Let me iron it at least."

He shook his head, as at some child's folly. "In a hundred miles, what's the difference?"

The clock struck the half hour.

"What time is it?"

She knew very well which half hour it was, but to be busy, to be serving him, she trotted into the other room and stared the clock in the face. "Five-thirty," she reported, breathless.

"About ready?"

For a moment she stood there staring at him, dizzied by the question, and then she realized, "Supper? Yes!" and began carrying the platters and bowls in. There was an empty tumbler by his place for the whiskey, but he chose tea instead, pouring again and again from the dewy pitcher with its floating lemon slices and cracked ice. He ate from every dish but the cornbread.

"Just something about it remembers me of bad times," he said, scowling.

She banished the plate of cornbread to the kitchen, out of his sight. So restless she was with her attentions—but never a bother, never distracting, never deprecating just to win compliments in return—she hardly ate at all. Her eyes brightened to see his appetite. He finished off on seconds—peach cobbler.

Right there at the table, his hat on the floor beside him, he tied on his tie, knotting that narrow bit of mourning at his throat. When it was in place, the old masking sadness returned to his face, but there was a light in his eyes now, they were open and clear, and there was an unbeaten expression to his lips under that shag of concealing gold straw.

Six struck.

"Wha' do you say?" He stood and stretched, left,

right, to the floor, retrieving his hat on the return trip, setting it deep on his damp hair. She laid off her apron, took up the keys to the car. The shadows were long around the house. The white paint was almost blue in the shade. An hour till the sun set behind the eclipsing mountains. It was cooler already.

She was backing the car when he remembered something important and got out, without even waiting for her to stop. If she had hurt him! Wanting to help him and hurting him! But he waved off her concern and ran back with her house keys and in and out again, swinging the whiskey bottle in his hand. He hadn't been inside long enough to drink, and he didn't drink now; she was glad. She took that as a tribute to her cooking and hospitality; he didn't need it now, the way he had.

He rode with his hat pushed back, exposing a white strip of forehead to the slanting sun as he clipped his nails with pocket nippers; left-hand nails very short, right-hand long and blunt. When they got to the fairgrounds, he directed her through the gates of privilege, to where the performers parked. She pulled in next to his station wagon.

Bud and Neal were already there. They gave a yelp and looked relieved when they spotted Lovingood. He got out and handed the bottle to Bud and leaned back in the open door to say, "Thanks for the groceries," his eyes cordial. He looked fine. No longer that abandoned-house stare. He shut the door and began discussing changes in the agenda. They hauled out their instrument cases, edgy, joking, checking the time.

Neal suggested starting with "Wildwood Flower," tapping his harp against his hand, staring through the reeds to the swallow-twittering sky. "We had a special request."

"If the others haven't done it by the time we go on,"

Lovingood said. Then, thinking it over: "Hell, let's do it anyway. They can't come close to us; we're the ones."

She waited a moment, listening to them talk, but she didn't fit in there, so she started back up the drive toward the music hall, toward the general admission stile. Lovingood caught up to her, swerved her back to a nearer entrance, to the one she had exited onto that afternoon, the one without steps. He gave Bud his banjo and took her in his arms, lifted her up in his restored strength and set her on the platform among the stagehands.

"Take care of her, boys," he said, and left her to them. They found her a seat near the front, in the reserved section. Proud, she kept her eyes on her lap, wondering what people were thinking.

Lovingood and company came on fifth that night. Well-received. She thought his playing was even better than before. He wore that same concentrating look, a haunted look, but was not haggard anymore. She took credit for that, for every note, for every movement of those hands as they flicked, crabbed, drummed, strummed, picked, tickled, hammered, chimed, wrung the notes from the banjo, making it talk, making it sing, making it mourn. The hour passed quickly, quickly. The crowd screamed for more, and this time Lovingood returned for an encore.

Afterward, she made her way up the aisle to the lobby. She ordered coffee poured over ice; her head ached. She stood sipping, as the PA blared from four corners of the room about the tables set up for the sale of albums and tapes and shirts and other souvenirs. Despite the PA, despite the general lobby racket, the shuffling and chatter of latecomers, the whining of children at the refreshment stand, she thought she recognized Lovingood's slow drawl, somewhere behind her, but when she turned, in the crowd, it seemed the whole world stood between them, shoulder to shoulder. From the hall came the amplified, wall-shaking beat of progressive, as a band played "Eight More Miles to Louisville." Traditionalists staggered out into the lobby, white-faced, shaking their heads, rubbing their ears.

She kept struggling across the lobby, against the general current, just one more anonymous body in the throng, born to blend in . . . There he was!

His back was to her, his body sheltering the phone on the wall as though trying to guard some precious tiny flame from being forever extinguished by the breeze of the passersby. His left hand with its opal ring lay flat against the wall, supporting him. He dropped a quarter in; she stopped when she saw him dialing a number off the little scrap of paper that the girl had handed up to him that afternoon, that scented note that had passed from hand to hand like contagion. His gritty baritone said, "Sugar? It's Edmun . . . Lovingood . . . Wha' do you say?" Listening to her, he scratched his sideburn; he laughed. He said, "Hell, honey, I don't have to be in Texas for three days . . ."

He didn't see her. She turned and fled, out the ticket gate and up the graveled road to the terraces where the car had been parked earlier. In her agitation she forgot that she had parked in the VIP lot, so she wandered from terrace to terrace in the strange alienating light of the dusk-to-dawns. Finally, she recollected herself and made her way back down the hill. She took the first empty seat, on the back row, under the sound booth, panting like a deer with a moment's respite from the harrying dogs.

Down front, Jim and Jesse were on. All in white, good guys. Their images twinned in her unfocused eyes—

they became a quartet. Their brilliant suits flared and swam in her mind; they were burned in on the backs of her lids. Their songs were old, new, endlessly repetitive, indistinguishable to her shuttered ears. They whined, wailed, glib in heartbreak, earnest in joy. She breathed deeply, letting her heartbeat settle. She grew quiet inside. In all that heat, her hands and feet were cold. She told herself, It's all right; you're all right.

Jim and Jesse finished and stepped back from the mikes, began taking their bows. The man sitting next to her hauled at her arm to drag her to her feet for an ovation, shouting, "Honey? Are you deaf? Come *on!* Ain't going to get any better till you get to heaven!" So she stood, with all the others, for the tribute.

Afterward, the crush of fans bore her on. Horrified, she saw that they were propelling her toward the souvenir tables, where she could already see Bud and Neal, down the line, presiding over the crates of Lovingood's music. Smarting, stupefied, afraid, she did not go farther. She stood numbly fingering the stacked T-shirts and autographed photos. After the crowd thinned she made her way to the VIP parking lot. She kept to the shadows till she could be sure— Lovingood's station wagon was gone.

She drove home fast, as though fleeing something, over the same dark empty roads, in the same ruts, the same dust rising and falling behind her. As she turned into her own driveway, she realized: He doesn't even know my name! It struck her as funny; she laughed.

She had all those pans to wash; all the while she laughed. And at first it *was* funny. Later she was sorry. And later still (this took some time) she was not sorry anymore.

Solomon's Seal

When they were courting, her people warned her, but she knew better. Who had kept them in meat through the Hoover years? With his rabbit boxes and early mornings, he was a man already, guarding a man's politics and notions, and like a mountain, wearing his own moody climate, one she prospered in. He brought the rabbits to her mother's kitchen window and held them up by the hind legs, swinging them like bells. When he skinned them and dressed them, she watched his quick knife as though learning. But she never did.

How they started out, that was how they wound up: on the same half-acre, in the same patched cabin. He was no farmer. Anything that grew on that red clay was *her* doing. After a few years she had cleared the stones from the sunny higher ground, piling them in a terrace, backfilling with woods dirt she gathered in flour sacks on her walks. She planted strawberries there. In the red clay of the garden she grew beans in the corn, peas, tomatoes, and bunching onions an uncle had given her as a wedding present. Some years, when the rains favored, she grew squash and mush-melons, the sweet little ones like baby heads.

They never had children. They never lacked dogs.

He kept a pen full of coon dogs and spent the nights with them in the moonlight, running them, drinking with his friends, unmending the darns she had applied to his overalls. He was a careless man. He had a way of waiting out her angers, a way of postponing things by doing something else just as necessary. So she postponed a few things too. She didn't even unpack her trunk filled with linens and good dishes her mama and aunts had assembled for her. They had practically blinded themselves sewing white on white, making that coverlet, but it was yellowed now, in its original folds, deep in the napthaed heart of her hope chest. What was the use of being house-proud in a house like that? She decided it was good enough for him to eat off oilcloth. She decided he didn't care if his cup matched his saucer, and if he didn't care, why should she? She decided after a time to give as good as she got, which wasn't much. The scarcity of it, and her continuous mental bookkeeping, set her face in a mask and left her lips narrowed. She used to sing to him, before they could afford a radio. Now he had the TV on, to any program, it didn't matter which, and watched it like a baby watches the rustling leaves of a tree, to kill a little time between feedings. She didn't sing to him anymore. She didn't sing at all. But she talked to her plants like they were people.

Sometimes he thought maybe there was company in the yard, and he'd move to the window to see if a man had come to buy one of his dogs. But it was only her. He'd give the wall a knock with the side of his fist, just to let her know he was listening.

"I'm praying," she'd say, without looking up from where she was pouring well water from a lard pail onto the newest seedlings.

"Witch," he'd mutter, and go back to his TV.

She had the whole place covered by now; she was always bringing in new plants, little bothersome herbs she warned him against stepping on in his splayed boots as he stumbled along the trails she had outlined in fieldstones. The paths narrowed as she took more and more room for her pretties. It was like a child's game, where he could or could not step. And what were they anyway but weeds? Not real flowers, like his mama had grown. He told her that often enough. He'd been all over that lot and had never seen one rose. Sometimes he stopped at the hardware store and lifted a flat of petunias to his nose, but they weren't like the ones he remembered, they didn't smell like anything. He asked her about it, asked if she reckoned it was the rockets and satellites. She knew better. She blamed it on the dogs.

She blamed his dogs for stinking so you couldn't smell cabbage cooking. The health department ought to run him in, she said. He said if she called them she'd wind up in hell faster than corn popping. She said if he cut across the lower terrace one more time he'd be eating through a vein in his arm till his jaw healed, if ever. When he asked what she was so mad about, she couldn't for the life of her remember, it was a rage so old.

The madder she got, the greener everything grew, helped along, in the later years, by the rabbit manure. He was too old now to run rabbits in the field. And the land had changed, built up all around, not like it used to be. So he rigged up cages at home and raised rabbits right there. Then it was rabbits and dogs and TV and his meals and that was his whole life. That and not stepping on her plants.

He removed the spare tire from the trunk of the Dodge and fastened it to the roof of the car. In the extra space, and after taking off the trunk lid, he built a dog box. He started carrying his better hounds to the field trials and she went along too, for the ride. Everywhere they went she managed to find a new plant or two. She kept a shovel in the back seat, and potato-chip bags or cut-off milk jugs to bring the loot home in. They'd ride along, not speaking, or speaking both at once, her about the trees, him about the dogs, not hearing the one thing they were each listening their whole life for.

Sometimes she drank too. Sometimes, bottle-mellowed, they turned to each other in that shored-up bed, but afterward things were worse somehow, and he'd go off the whole next day to visit with other cooners, and she'd walk for miles in the woods, seeking wake-robin or Solomon's seal. She always dug at the wrong time, or too shallow, or something. For a few hours it would stand tall as it had grown, but the color would slowly fade, and with it her hopes. She'd be out there beside it, kneeling, talking to it softly, when he'd drive in, red-faced, beery. He'd see her turned back and head on up to the kennel to stand a few minutes, dangling his hands over the fence at the leaping dogs.

Forty years like that. It surprised her very much when he told her he wanted a divorce. He had been in the hospital a week and was home again. While he was in the hospital they told her not to upset him, so she held back the news. When he got home he found out that three of his whelps were sick and two more had already died. It was Parvo virus, locally epidemic, but the vet couldn't persuade him it wasn't somehow *her* fault. He spent the nights, sick as he still was, sitting up with the dogs, feeding them chicken soup from one of her saucepans. That was how the final argument started, her resenting that. If she really wanted to help him, he said, she'd just leave him alone. We'll see how you like that, she said, and took some clothes and went to her sister's. While she was there, a man came and served her with papers. He's crazy, is what he is, she said to the ferns; consider the source, she said to the laurel. He didn't want her? She knew better.

She used the rabbit's foot to rouge her cheeks, to add a little color. It surprised her, tying on her scarf to go to court, how much her face looked like his. The likeness was so sudden it startled her into a shiver. "Rabbit running over your grave," she said, thinking she was saying it to him.

There wasn't anything to the divorce. Uncontested, it was all over with very soon. But there was some heat over the division of property. He wound up with the house and she got the lot. He had custody of the dogs. He had six months to remove them and anything he wanted from the property, and after that he must stay away forever. He had the house moved in one piece. He hired a mover to come and load it onto a truck and haul it away. He set it up on a lot north of the river, among the pines, and in a few months he had pens for the dogs built alongside so he didn't have to walk far.

She bought a secondhand mobile home and moved it onto her lot when his six months were up. He had left things pretty well torn up; the housemovers had crushed and toppled her trellises and walls. She had weeks of work to right that. Even though it was all final, she was still afraid. She painted pieces of board with KEEP OUT and DO NOT DIG and nailed them to the trees. She tied scraps of rag to wires she ran from tree to tree, setting apart the not-to-be-trod-upon areas. She listened sharp, kept her radio tuned low, in case he was out there, coming back, like he used to, knocking over trash cans, beating on the door, crying, "It's me . . . Carl . . . let me in?"

But he didn't come back. She had no word of him at all, though she knew well enough where he was living, like some wild thing, deep in the woods with his hounds. Sometimes she saw his car going down the main road, it couldn't be missed, with that funny dog crate nailed in the trunk and the spare tire on the roof. She could watch the road from the hilltop as she stood at her clothesline. He drove as slow as always. It maddened her to see him go by so slow, as though he were waiting for her to fling herself down the hill headlong, to run after him crying, "Carl! Come back!" She wouldn't. She went on with her laundry. The old towel she picked up from the basket next was so bleach-burned it split in two when she snapped it. She hung the pieces on the line between her and the road, turned her back, picked up her basket, and headed for her trailer, down the hill, where he couldn't see her, though she knew how he drove, never looking left or right, even when she rode along with him, not turning his head one inch in her direction as he went on and on about the dogs. No more neck than a whale.

She was at the post office buying a money order when she heard he had remarried. She knew that couldn't be true. It wasn't a reliable source. She asked around. Nobody knew. She let it get to her, she couldn't rest just thinking of it. She didn't care; if she just knew *for sure*, that was it. "He's seventy-two years old," she said. Meaning: who could stand him but his dogs? She was out raking leaves from the main path when she decided to go see for herself. She finished up in her garden and changed to a clean shirt. She walked out to the store and phoned Yubo to come take her. Yubo was planting Miss Hamilton's garden, always did plant beans on Good Friday, and he wouldn't be there right away. She said as soon as possible, and stood at the store waiting. It gave her time to think over what she was going to say when she got there. She knew where it was; she'd been by there once, just to see how it looked, had held her pocketbook up to shield her face in case he happened to be there and noticing anybody going by. Not that he was a noticer. She drank Coca-Cola while she waited, and when Yubo came she almost said take me home, because the long wait and the walk in the sun and the whole project was making her dizzy. But she had come this far, and so had Yubo.

The house looked about the same as when it had been hers, except it stood on concrete blocks now instead of those shimmed-up rocks from the river. She told Yubo to wait. She walked down the drive to the door, which was open, unscreened, and she called, before she could think better, "I'm home," but of course she meant, "I'm here." Confused, she didn't say anything when the woman came out to see who it was. An old woman as big and solid as Carl, bare-armed, bright-eyed. One of the dogs was out of the pen, two of the dogs, and they were following right at her heels. They had the run of the house! The old woman sat on the steps and the dogs lay beside her, close enough so she could pet them as they panted against her bare feet. "Carl's not here," the old woman said.

"I was just passing by," she said, and turned to go to Yubo, who had the taxi backed around and waiting. It wasn't a real taxi, not a proper taxi, and it was considerably run down. Still, she slammed the door harder than necessary. The wind of its closing made the just-set-out petunias in the circle around the mailbox post shiver and nod.

At home, among her borders and beds, she worked all afternoon carrying buckets of water up the hill to slop onto her tomato seedlings, her pepper sets, her potato slips. She worked till she was so weary she whimpered, on her sofa, unable to rest. She fell asleep and had a bad dream. Someone had come and taken things. She woke herself up to go check. She locked the door and moved the piled papers and canned goods off her hope chest and raised the lid. Everything she had held out against him all those years was there. She took the coverlet out and looked it over, as though someone might have stolen the French knots off it. Then she unwrapped the dishes, fine gold-rimmed plates. They weren't china, but they were good. She thought she heard someone. Startled, she turned quickly, knocking the plate against the trunk. The dish broke in two, exactly in two. She took up a piece in each hand and knelt there a long time, but the tears never came. Finally she said, "That's one he won't get," and the thought gave her peace. She broke all the others, one by one, and laid them back in the trunk. She kept the coverlet out. It would do to spread over her tomato plants; the almanac said there would be no more frost, but she knew better. There was always one last frost.

After staking the coverlet above her young plants, weighting it at the corners with rocks, she stooped to see how the Solomon's seal was doing. She had located it by its first furled shoots, like green straws, sticking up through the oak-leaf duff on one of her walks; had marked the place, going home for a bucket and pail, digging deep, replanting so it faced the same way to the sun. It had not dried out. It had good soil. But already it was dying. There was some little trick to it. "You'd think I could learn," she said. But she never did.

A Man Among Men

1

His old man lay in Grady Miller's best steel casket with the same determined-to-die look on his face that he had worn throughout his final two months of decline, from the night Olene had run red-eyed back through the Labor Day rain with his uneaten supper on its wilting picnic plate to report, "He's gone in that camper and put on his nightshirt and gone to bed. For keeps." She had shaken the rain from her jacket and scarf, using one of the green-checked napkins to dry her face. "He's talking funny. I don't like the way he's talking. Made me lay out his dark suit where he could see it and told me, 'No shoes, no use burying good leather, just see my socks are clean,' all because of a dog. A dog!"

"Daddy thought the world of Smokey Dawn," Thomas pointed out.

He and the old man had spent their entire holiday looking for the hound, as far south as Buck's Creek, all around the public hunting lands, calling, calling from the windows of the truck. She had never stayed out so long. She had never trashed in her life. From time to time the old man raised his arm and hissed, "Listen!", his bladey hand like an ax. Once it was the waul of a blue-tailed rooster, strutting in a dried cornfield; it almost sounded like the dog. The cock stepped toward them, icy eye taking it all in. "Shoot!" The old man fell back against the seat, disappointed. They drove on.

There was a strange feel to the weather; the sky was so overcast the morning glories in the corn were still open wide. "Weatherbreeder," the old man said, staring at the clouds, but he wasn't looking for rain. In a few miles he spotted them—three buzzards—freckles on the flannel belly of the afternoon. The old man tensed up and leaned forward, still hoping, and peered down the dirt lane to where she lay in the goldenrod. Before Thomas got the truck full-stopped, his daddy was scrabbling out. He thrashed his hat all around to keep the birds aloft. He still had that sense he was rescuing her. His tough old shoes barely cleared the dust as he hastened toward the corpse, stumbling over pebbles and lurching on, stiff-footed.

Thomas lagged back, letting him handle it. He lit his cheroot on the third match; there was an east wind, mean and cold, shaking the young pines. Handfuls of sparrows sifted themselves out of the blow, deeper and deeper into the thickets.

His daddy was shivering.

Thomas shed his jacket and offered it to the old man, who wasn't dressed for the knifing wind. He took it, knelt, and wrapped the dog in it. "I reckon it was her heart," he said, beating his parchment fist against his chest. "No bigger than a fiddle when I got me my first redbone pup, Billy Boy it was." He looked away as Thomas lifted the dog and carried her back to the truck. The old man walked alone, counting up his losses: "After Billy it was Babe . . . and Ginger Tom out of Babe and French Lou—she had the straightest legs of them all—

and Red Pearl and Rabbit Joe, one-eyed but it never cost him a coon, heart like a tiger . . . did I say Racing Joe? And Joe's Honey and Honey's Nan . . ." He flinched when Thomas slammed the tailgate: a solemn closing, the end of an era. They headed home. "And Jolly, and Honey's Nan, I mention her yet? And Prince Ego and Skiff. And Smokey," he said, "Smokey Dawn." He stared toward the darkening west, his eyes cold and gray as a dead-man's nickels. "Well, that's about it." They rode in silence then.

By the time Thomas parked, at home, the old man's interest had waned to a single, final point. "Dig it deep" was how he put it. "I don't want a plow turning her up some day." He headed for his mobile home and went in and closed the door.

When Olene saw the windbreaker over the dog's body, she said, "I'm not washing that in my machine."

"Dean's not home yet?"

"I'm not worried." She laughed. "When you're seventeen you run on nerve and Dr. Pepper, not Daylight Saving. You'll have to bury her yourself."

It was already raining—the first huge cold drops— when he went to get the mattock.

Olene had never had much patience with the old man's sulks. "Do something," she said, after supper, just as the phone rang. She went on scraping the old man's untouched food into the garbage. "Turned his head to the wall, not one bite would he taste, and me on my feet chopping and cooking since noon." All the time Thomas was on the phone she kept reciting her welling grievances at his back. She broke off when he reached for his uniform jacket on its hook.

"Now what?"

He zipped the jacket to his chin, then unzipped it halfway; he dug out his truck keys and clipped his beeper to his belt. "A car hit a deer on the quarry road."

"Couldn't someone else?"

He unlocked the cabinet and took down his service revolver. "I had last weekend off, remember?"

"We didn't do anything."

He loaded the gun and clicked it shut. "I'll just step on across and check on Daddy before I go." Lightning showed the walk to be running like a brook. "And it's not a camper," he said as he plunged out into the deluge.

He splashed across the flagstones to the mobile home. The windows were open; it was cave-damp and dark inside. The wet curtains dragged at his hands as he cranked the jalousies shut. He turned on the lights and ran the thermostat up. At the bedroom door he hesitated. "It's Thomas," he announced softly.

"Come on."

Thomas took the old man's hand and clasped it; it was cold. His daddy puzzled him out a feature at a time from his pillows. He shook his head; they were strangers. "I recollect you now," he bluffed. "We were running Blue Jolly and Nan . . ." He trailed off, uncertain. "That old coon—tail shot off four years back—no fight left in her, no fight. So fat she dropped into the dogs and just let 'em rip. No play in the pack for that. Funny . . ." He yawned for breath. "Funny . . ." He opened his eyes and stared all the way through Thomas, clear out the other side into the young century when someone, someone . . .

"*Who?*" he asked irascibly. He focused again, present tense. "My memory's shot to chow," he confessed. He glanced indifferently around the room, recognizing nothing but his suit on the chair. "I'm checking out of here," he announced abruptly, flailing himself upright, then falling back, exhausted. "You help me, mister?"

Thomas nodded.

"You notify my son, Little Earl—Earl Teague, Jr.— on the Star Route . . ." He gestured with his thumb, south.

Thomas watched the pulse wriggle in the old man's temple. Was he just sulking, like Olene said? Or was it another of the little strokes that left him more and more a stranger?

"Daddy?" Thomas said, sharp, calling the cloudy eyes back into focus.

Frowning, he examined Thomas' face and resumed, "Highly thought of . . . in the book . . . look him up . . . Earl Teague, Jr. He'll come take care of me."

"But what about Thomas?" Thomas asked, for the record.

The old man seemed to have dozed off.

"Daddy?"

He blinked awake. "Who is it?"

"Thomas."

"Not him," he said, irritated. He had never suffered fools gladly. "He's dead." He looked at Thomas and yawned.

You son of a bitch, Thomas thought. He wanted to shake the old man, wake him, make claims. But what was the use of that now? Or ever? When Little Earl was killed by the train, hadn't his daddy stared at Thomas standing by the closed coffin and asked, "Why couldn't it have been you?"

That was when Thomas knew.

2

His old man lay in Grady Miller's front parlor be- tween the adjustable lamps casting their discreet

40-watt pink-of-health upon him head and foot. He was dressed in his Sunday best. Olene had tucked a rose into his lapel. She came up to Thomas standing there and ran her arm through his. "Isn't he sweet?" she said, giving the little bouquet of buds and baby's breath a pat, smoothing the streamers across the old man's chest. GRANDDADDY was spelled out in press-on gold letters on the satin ribbon. She had ordered that, in Dean's name. The boy hadn't seen the old man since the last week of the hospital stay, when life-support was all that tethered him to the world. He hadn't seen him dying, and he hadn't seen him dead. Thomas' simmering resentment of that finally boiled over on Saturday night when Dean came in late for supper, said he wasn't hungry, and announced that the clutch had torn out of his Chevy again.

"Ten days!" Thomas said. "This time it lasted ten days!"

"Three weeks," Olene corrected. She looked it up in the checkbook. "He can drive mine."

"He won't need it; he's coming with us," Thomas said.

"I can fix it myself in three hours if I get the parts."

"Not tonight." Thomas finished his coffee, standing. He set the cup in the sink.

"I'm not going down there."

"Your granddaddy—"

"Is dead and I'm not. I'm sure as hell not," Dean said. He laughed. He drank what was left of the quart of milk right from the carton. When Thomas backhanded him, it knocked his sunglasses and the empty milk carton across the kitchen. One of the lenses rolled over by the trash.

"No!" Olene stepped between.

"I'd beat his ass till it turned green if I thought it would do any good," Thomas said, over her head. Still he couldn't see into the boy's eyes. How long had it been since they *saw* each other? He turned away, shrugged off Olene's restraining hand. In the silence, which prolonged, the boy wiped the milk mustache off with his fist.

When Olene saw the look on his face, she said, "He's just trying to raise you."

"All he raises is objections," Dean said.

Thomas headed up the stairs, two at a time, to shave and dress for the wake. "Don't wait up," Dean bragged as he left. He took Olene's car.

It was the first time he had stayed out all night that they didn't know where to find him.

On Sunday morning (the old man's funeral would be that afternoon) the beeper summoned Thomas on a dead-body call. He left Olene and the men's Bible class on honor guard at Miller's and headed across town to Doc Daniels' pharmacy. Doc was the one who had spotted the body in the weeds, followed the footprints from his broken-in back door out through the frost and down the gullied fill-dirt specked with soda cans and gum wrappers. Doc had called, "Hey! HEY!", a wake-up call, in case it was sleep and not death he had been stalking, but when he got close enough to be fairly sure he hurried back to the phone to spread the news. The EMS driver got there first and made a tentative diagnosis—overdose—but now they were waiting on the coroner and Thomas to arrive.

When Thomas got there, Doc led the way again, down the clay bank, his white bucks getting pinker with every dusty step. Thomas was in a hurry; Doc caught at his sleeve to stay apace. He was panting to keep up. Together they leaped the last gully. All the way Doc was telling, telling, fixing his magnified gaze on Thomas' profile.

"Look at him," Doc accused, as they came to the corpse.

A boy, curling a bit toward the fetal pose, lay on his left side. For a moment Thomas thought he knew him—a trick of the mind after a sleepless night—dirty sneakers, faded jeans, blue windbreaker, watch cap. He swayed, rubbed his eyes, then knelt for a closer look, resting his hand on the boy's stiff, angled knees.

Behind him Doc was saying, "This makes the sixth time I've been robbed. I've got payments to make like anyone else—"

Thomas searched the boy's pockets for ID. He flipped through the haggard wallet. Doc leaned forward, squinting. "So who gets the bad news?" he wondered.

Thomas stood up. "I'll tell them," he said, and started up the bank to his truck. He took the time to smoke one of his little cigars. He answered no questions. The crowd moved back to let his truck pass. He drove fast though there was no hurry.

He crossed the tracks at midtown and turned right onto a forgotten road hardly more than an alley paralleling the rails. He headed south till the paving turned to gravel; it peppered the underside of his truck as he negotiated the lane's washboard heaves and hollows. He rolled his window up against the dust rather than slow down.

The road dead-ended in a grove of blighted elms beyond a bare yard, clean-swept with a broom in that country way of deterring snakes. Mazes of rabbit fence held back the frost-nipped remains of faded petunias. On the staggering mailbox, in descrescendo, red paint not a season old announced ELSiE BLANd beneath the former tenant's name, shoeblacked out. A dingy cat leaped up onto the truck hood, settled on the cab roof, and held aloof from Thomas' hand. From the grayed house came the sound of fast sad blues, decades old, scratchy—an ancient, sturdy record salvaged from attic or rummage sale. Before Thomas crossed the porch the music sped up to 78 rpm; people were laughing. They didn't hear him.

He knocked again. Louder.

A laughing woman materialized behind the rusty rump-sprung screen door, wiping her eyes with her fingers and shaking the tears away. "Sounds like mice in them cartoons," she explained. She leaned into the dark to call, "Jude? Jude! You shut that down now, *shut it*." To Thomas she said, "It's Sunday, I know, but I didn't reckon it'd hurt anything for him to listen. We been to church this morning, early." She guessed he was a preacher.

Because they did not know each other, because he had come in his pickup truck instead of the cruiser, because she did not notice the blue light on the dashboard behind the windshield reflecting October, because he was dressed for his daddy's funeral and wasn't in uniform, he could see she had no idea at all who or what he was. He held up his badge and said, "It's the Law, ma'am. I'm Tom Teague. Are you Mrs. Bland?" And because he had come on official business and there was more than courtesy conveyed in his manners—some additional intimation of apology for bad news, perhaps the worst news—the solemnity communicated itself through the rusty screen and into her heart instantly and flamed up into remorse, as though the fires of regret and grief had long been laid and awaited but the glint off Thomas' badge to kindle them.

"My boy Ben! Killed oversea in the service!" she screamed, voicing her oldest premonition, her dreams that woke her, brought her to her knees in the night-watch. She had a map of the world with Lebanon marked on it in ballpoint, circled and circled, to help her focus her prayers.

"No," Thomas said. He tried the door. It was latched. "Mrs. Bland . . ." he appealed. Something in his tone arrested her wild attention. The needle scratched loudly across the old record and resumed playing again, at proper speed, the fast sad blues. She settled her eyes on Thomas'.

Quieter, she said, "Then it's about Ray." She unhooked the screen and admitted trouble into her scrub-worn rooms. Every windowsill had its beard of green plants in foil-covered pots. Above the mantel with its clutter of photographs hung a lithograph of radiant Christ.

"Jude, honey," his mama suggested, "about time for your train."

Jude came in from the kitchen, a man who would be a boy all his life.

"We got to discuss," she told him. "You go on out." No introductions.

Passing by, the boy stuck out his hand to Thomas. "Pleased to," he said. The old ladies that Elsie cleaned for praised his manners and his willingness to climb ladders; they let him unclog their gutters for cookies and dimes.

The train at the town limits sounded its whistle. The boy hurried out to admire the pink Albert City Farmers grain cars rolling past on tracks not a city block away.

"Just a little something went wrong when he was borned, a good boy, no trouble, not like Ray." Elsie breathed faster. She aimed her sharp nose at Thomas and angrily asked, "What about him? Tell me what he done."

"I'm afraid it's bad news, Mrs. Bland."

She thought it over. "Bound to be." She pushed herself up out of the chair and fetched one of the photographs from the mantel. She handed it to Thomas. Its cheap metal frame was cold and sharp as a knife. There was the face of the boy Doc had found in the weeds. Thomas cleared his throat. He handed the picture back; for a moment they both held it, then he let it go.

"He's dead," he told her. There was nothing to tell but the truth, and it only took two words. Thomas thought that was how he would want to hear it, if he ever had to. Elsie heard it, Thomas thought, without surprise. She seemed stupefied, though, and it was a minute before she repeated, "Dead." She sat staring at the photograph in her lap.

"He's the one like his pappy," she specified. She just sat there. Silent.

"You'll want to ask me some questions," Thomas suggested.

Elsie looked out the window at Jude. "He purely loves them trains. Don't miss a one. Always try to locate near the tracks for him."

Georgia, Clinchfield, and West Point stock rolled past, slowing, and the British Columbia car with its magnolia logo stopped directly in view as the L&N engines switched back and forth uptown, shunting a feed car aside.

"He's the good one," Elsie said. Canny, she studied Thomas' face, reading there her familiar, bitter lesson. "Ray done bad?" she guessed. She set the photograph back in its place on the mantel. "You don't love them for it, but you love them. There's good in between the bad times." She smoothed a wrinkle in the mantel runner, chased the fold ahead of her fingers to the fringed end, then chased it again.

The train, readying itself for the run north through the deep cuts and poplar hills, revved its engines until the whole house rumbled, making itself felt in every bone.

"The Lloyd Jesus knows I love all my boys!" she cried, her face lifted to the calendar Christ as she wept. When she was calmer she wiped her face on her apron and took her seat again, her tear-shining hands inert on the arms of her chair, her swollen feet in their strutted oxfords braced heel by heel for the truth. "All right," she consented. She sniffed deeply, inhaling the last of her tears. "You tell me what it is. What'll be in them newspapers. Tell me in so many words. I don't want to read about it." Her voice was worn down with speaking up for herself and her sons, husky from making itself heard over mill racket, muffled by sorrows. "I hate to read about it," she explained, then cleared her throat with a sigh and waited.

That was when Thomas, though it wasn't his intention, admitted, "It could have been my own son. I thought it was."

3

His old man lay in Grady Miller's lifetime-guaranteed burial vault, and the mourners—those windblown few who waited for the closing and the anchoring of their wreaths in the raw clay—drifted like dark leaves against the whited wall of Soul's Harbor Church. Olene's sinuses were acting up; she couldn't wear a hat over that hairdo and she had left her scarf in her other coat. She withdrew to the sanctuary of the darkened church itself. Miller's assistants were already folding the chairs, rolling up the fake grass, loading the pulleys and frame and plush seat covers into their van. The pastor gave Thomas a little tap with his Bible as he went by, saying, "We'll keep in touch," and headed briskly for his car. His wife was already buckled in, ready.

There came that general, genteel exodus, with no backward glances, as life went on. The road and margins cleared of traffic and then it was so quiet; there was only the flutter of the canopy's scalloped canvas as the wind rocked it on its moorings. The grave-diggers' words were blown far afield, toward the kneeling cattle, fawn-colored jerseys, on the distant hill. They looked legless; they reminded Thomas of that deer on the quarry road Labor Day night, her front legs sheared in the accident, yet somehow she was still alive.

He had knelt beside her. Her doe eye, widely dilated, stared vacantly up at the sky, her nostrils flaring with each quick breath. She was dying, and it was taking too long.

"Where the hell is the Ranger?"

The inevitable crowd had begun to gather. G.W. Laney, first responder, stamped and snorted like a dray beast. He was a volunteer, whose wife had given him an emergency light for his birthday. Its intermittent red sweep refreshed his sunburn and turned the rain to blood. His scanner spat static. Thomas had a headache. He and G.W. laid a tarp over the deer.

"Back 'em up," Thomas told him, and G.W. herded the bystanders deeper into the dark. "Appreciate y'all coming, folks, but how about clearing on off for home now?" They mostly went. Thomas couldn't see how the deer was still alive. He checked her again, ran his hand down her neck.

"I'm not waiting," he decided.

At the gunshot, the door of the ditched car ratcheted

open and a young man climbed uphill out into the downpour. Thomas stared. They hadn't told him it was Dean! The boy had a bloody handkerchief tied around his left palm. They stood in the rainy circle of flashlight and Thomas asked, first off, "Whose car have you wrecked this time?"

"Ginnie let me drive. You know Ginnie—Doc Daniels' daughter."

The kind you find dead in a ditch some day, Thomas thought, watching her get out now, her jacket held over her head to keep the rain off her bright hair. Her T-shirt advertised Squeeze Me, I'm Fresh. She sided with Dean, facing Thomas down, two against one.

"It's totaled," Thomas said, surveying the wrecked sedan.

"I'm insured," Ginnie said. "But still I bet Daddy'll shit a brick." She laughed. Dean started to laugh, then didn't. Then did. Ginnie flicked a few tiny cubes of safety glass off his shoulder.

"You been drinking?" Thomas asked, officially. And unofficially.

"Naw, uh, just beer. Just one." Dean shut his eyes, stood on tiptoe, and began touching first one index finger, then the other, to his nose. "See?"

"You need a doctor?" Thomas kept his voice casual as he eyed that blood-blackened bandage.

"It's just a cut." Dean was exhilarated by the adrenalin. "Damn deer bust right out on me! Like a bomb. Clean through the windshield." He avoided looking at that mound under the rain-glittering tarp.

"How fast were you going?" Thomas shone the flashlight along the pavement. "Where'd you brake?"

"You saying it's my fault?" The boy's raw fist in its bandage tightened.

"I'm saying what I'd say to anyone."

Dean crossed his arms over his chest when he heard that and bent a hot, hurt look on his father—part anger, part disappointment—as though he had been handed a stone instead of bread.

Thomas knew that look well enough. "Sue me," he told the boy. The wrecker was backing up to Ginnie's car and the Ranger had arrived, with a notebook to fill with facts. He began asking Dean and Ginnie the hard questions. When he finished and had no charges to file, Thomas offered, "Y'all need a lift?"

Ginnie said, that quick, "We're going with G.W.," and G.W. grinned, because he hadn't asked them and because Ginnie was like that, fixing things to suit her. (She had a way of daring him that sent Dean diving off the rocky cliff over the reservoir at least once a summer, risking his neck for one moment of her laughter, and before the peony of spray had settled around him, before he had surfaced, she was bored, thinking up something else. Thomas had warned them off those rocks, but Ginnie was worth the risk, worth the slow climb back up the cliff to her lacquered toes.) She swung herself up into G.W.'s front seat and Dean got in back.

"Keep it between the ditches," Thomas had called as they rolled off, white water fluming up from beneath the wide tires of the Jeep.

"How much longer?" Thomas wondered. He had objected to the machine, backfilling, so the men were shoveling by hand.

One of the mourners, with an estimating glance over toward the undertaker's canopy, said, "*Now,* I think. They're about done." The grave was covered and the wreaths were being laid. The ribbons rattled in the wind.

Thomas led the way, alone. Friends who had stayed

set out in a broken rank behind him, by twos and threes, across the intervening graves, picking their way around the minimal obstacles of granite and marble, not talking. The throaty mufflers of Dean's orange Chevy caught their attention from the moment he rounded the curve by Foster's store. He burned a week's worth of rubber off its tires and stopped in a scour of gravel at the foot of the hill. Thomas turned to watch. They all did.

Dean had a bucket of bronze mums. He came on fast, loping across the field, hurdling the cemetery wall, catching up. They made way for him, but still he hung back, only stepping up to set the flowers at the headstone, between his grandparents' graves. Then he rested on Little Earl's footstone, catching his breath. He had nothing to say when they greeted him. Sullen, he raised the hood of his jogging suit and tied it snug, but they could still see his black eye. He stood suddenly and stamped his foot. "Cramp," he explained, doing some exercises to stretch the kink from his calf. "Gotta work it out." He jogged off east across the field, over unclaimed ground, then down toward the gravel pit, and around again.

As they watched him go, one of the men said, "Give him time, Tom, he's just a kid." That was what Olene was always saying. But wasn't that what everyone had said about Little Earl? Wild as sunspots and dead at twenty-four after losing a race with a locomotive, and not a day in that whole wasted life had he ever thought of anyone but himself.

The others paid their last respects to the old man, calling him a man among men, shaking Thomas' hand, and heading on down the hill to their cars. The diggers, behind the church, loaded their backhoe onto its trailer, threw in their handtools, and drove off.

When they had gone, Dean trotted back. "I wasn't going to come," he said. He pulled up his left sock, then stood not quite facing his daddy. They were alone now.

"You just about missed it," Thomas agreed. Why had he bothered to come? Thomas couldn't look at him, at that bruised eye. Had he hit him *that* hard? Where the hell had he been all night?

"Your mother was worried sick," Thomas said. He fumbled with his matches. Dean didn't say anything, as usual, just looked around. "She's in the church," Thomas told him. The boy shrugged.

"You're the ones who let the air out of the cruiser's tires, aren't you? You and Ginnie." He'd figured that out in fifteen seconds. Did they think he was a fool?

"Sue me," Dean said. Thomas blinked when he heard himself quoted. The boy stepped up to the curb of the plot and balanced on his toes, taller than his daddy, then stepped back down. "I was pissed," he said.

Before Thomas could decide if that was an apology, the door of the church skreeked open, then slammed. Olene stood on the steps, her eyes shaded by her upheld hands as she stared their way. She waved and shouted something, but the wind scattered her words. She gave up, but stayed out, as though she wanted to keep an eye on them. She sat on the top step in what was left of the sun, hugging her cold knees.

"And leave Ginnie out of it," Dean added.

"I figured it was you." Thomas unpocketed his fists to stoop and right a spray of carnations the wind had tipped over. The shoulders of his suit were white from leaning against the chalky shingles of the church. The scent of dying flowers choked him. Just that mere whiff made him remember all the other times, but he didn't want to remember. A phoebe settled hard, rocking a little on the rusty gate, feebly singing. Thomas concentrated on the bird.

When he caught Dean looking at him, he nodded toward the boy's car and said, "You fixed the clutch." He was getting hoarse.

"Yeah." Dean almost smiled.

The wind was strong enough to lean on, like it would never die. Dean glanced at his watch and sighed. He held out his hand, signaling *five minutes more* to Olene, waiting.

Thomas crossed his arms. "Don't let me keep you."

One by one Dean popped the knuckles of both hands, taking his time. Thomas hated that. "You going to stay out here all night?" Dean asked.

"Look who's talking."

"At least I was warm," Dean said.

Thomas checked the sky. "This time it didn't rain. It always rains." He watched the blue pickup truck bump across Langford's far pasture, and the cows begin walking toward the hay in back. One of the calves bawled and ran to catch up with its mother.

Olene came across the cemetery, making careful steps in her high heels, holding her coat shut. "Thomas?" she called. She lurched, stopped, and removed her shoes, then came on, faster, over the grass. "I'd rather have pneumonia than broken bones," she said. She looked from Thomas to Dean and back again. Thomas took her shoes and put them in the pockets of his suitcoat. She reached up to touch Dean's bruised eye, but he pulled away.

Olene knelt to gather up the remains of the everlasting and lilies she had planted. "Look what they did," she said. The careless mower in his zeal had laid them low. The diggers had chipped the granite corner monogram and snubbed the rose, the only volunteer. Thomas toed a stray clod from his daddy's footstone, which was already in place, part of the package deal when they buried his mother.

"All they've got to do is cut the date of death," Olene said, bending to tap the cold stone. "It's been a while, but they can match Mama Teague's numbers exactly." Olene dusted her hands and hugged her coat tighter to her. "I'm freezing to death," she said. "I'll be next."

"We'll go," Thomas said. Olene ran on and got into Thomas' truck and shut the door, but Dean stayed. Thomas was shivering. He made a giveaway gesture at the ground: farewell. "Maybe Mama can do something with him," he said. "I sure as hell never could."

The phoebe on the iron gate flew out and back, out and back, preying and preening. The wind had finally let up, and for a moment there was no other motion in the world but the lone bird, weakly singing. Then Dean stepped across Little Earl's grave and brushed the chalk dust off Thomas' shoulders, brushed and brushed.

That was when Thomas began to cry.

A Country Girl

The Misses Bliss kept store north of the limits, a mile past the FFA sign that said Welcome Back when you were going south and Come Again when you were going north, although if you were to stop and ask them the way to Rydal, the one would be sure to smile in pardon of the question while the other would gently reply, "You're now in town." There was not an uninhabited front porch in all the valley on any summer afternoon, so you could inquire for directions all along if you were lost and someone would be sure to tell you, "Rydal is the center of the universe," and it might be that a barefoot girl with a flat-top guitar would stare coolly past you and her uncle, propped against the post hollowed by carpenter bees, would say nothing, having vowed long before not to speak to anyone, not even kin, till suppertime. The dogs, bellying low on the under-porch shadows, would be saving their energy for moonrise along the river. You could pick up one of the little early apples from the ground and eat it right then without worrying about pesticide.

The most famous local citizen was hanged just that much before a reprieve—a sad, legendary thing; there's a farm named for him, and grandchildren. And the second-most-famous person, the lady writer, is dead nearly as long as the hanged man, and buried in her chapel garden beside her daughter Faith. Not that many pilgrims seek the grave anymore. And the house she loved wears antennae, and a twin-engine fiberglass cruiser on its trailer is parked on the terrace where the doctor, who had a presentiment, told her, taking into account the flowered borders, the wide fields, the view: "You have everything but time."

The barefoot girl by now will have finished her singing, not the impersonal, brave gospel singing, but melodies low and private as lullaby. She will have set the guitar aside with a slight discord. And she will sigh, wanting nothing in the world she can name, free to come and go with no more than a lift of her tanned hand, yet burdened, restless, seeking that one thing to strike out at or from. Soon the afternoon train will track across the valley and the colt in Paul Lilley's pasture will race it, pleasant to see. The girl would go that way. There was no hurry.

But when she got there, there were others.

"I live," said the man with the camera, "where you can hear alligators groaning each night in the tidal mud."

The license plate on the car said Sunshine State, sure enough, but that didn't mean there was no rain in Florida, or liars either. The girl shook her head, slightly, in rebuke, the fair hair swaying and settling into order on her shoulders.

"It's true, every word," his wife corroborated, dabbing a dry brush on her canvas. (But you cannot prove alligators by protestation.) How could they say such things in Paul Lilley's pasture and every cricket and June bug singing born two thousand feet above sea level, thereabouts?

"That's all right," the girl told them kindly.

The woman had painted the colt. The train had been too much for her. So the dappled horse ran alone at the back of her perspective, presentably drawn.

"That's how I like," the girl told her. The man with the camera checked his watch again.

"Mother," he said. The sun was in decline.

"I know, I know," his wife sighed, folding up shop. She released the wet canvas from the easel and admired it briefly. "Oh, well, I guess you got the real action with your camera."

"Two different arts. Two different artists. Two separate truths," he said easily, as though he usually talked that way. He cluttered their picnic things into the hamper and recorked the Pontet-Latour.

"You keep this." The woman handed the girl the painting.

"Oh, no, I caint, I mustn't."

"Whyever not?"

The girl frowned in concentration, seeking the exact ethic being jeopardized. "We don't make uneven exchanges."

The man and woman looked at each other in amusement. He got in the car.

"But I want you to have it," the painter protested. "Find something (quick!) to exchange."

The girl drew a deep breath. "Poor Wayfarer," she said, then announced her name, "Elizabeth Inglish," and began to sing a cappella in her low, thrilling way. When she finished, she received the painting from the woman, and they drove away.

"Mercy! I never expected a serenade." The woman snapped her seat belt. Looking back once, she saw the girl still standing there with the painting raised to her eyes as a sunshade.

"Country girl," he said, like a slide caption. Before

the dust behind them had settled, they had digested her into anecdote.

The Bliss sisters had directed him here, a stranger. He had their quavering map stuffed in his shirt pocket to keep it from blowing out the window as he rode along. He had no more country sense than to drive on the clay road like a turnpike. His brick-red wake stood tall as a two-story house, slowly settling grit onto whatever laundry happened to be hanging out and seeping into the crevices between the piano keys at the Missionary Baptist Church if Mavis Cole had left it open again after practicing the choir. Anybody who looked could tell some stranger was coming. But May Inglish wasn't looking, she was cooking for the reunion. Horace was at the barbershop swapping lies with the others, and Sophie and Bremen were playing in the branch. Uncle Billy was out in the corn, potting crows. Aunt Lila and them were due in the morning, soon enough. Uncle Cleveland was due any time, and welcome, but at his age you could never be sure. His chair to preside in was already set out in the shade of the beech tree, the sawhorses were aligned to make the picnic tables, and the white sheets for tablecloths were ironed and folded away on the sideboard by the piles of Chi-net platters and bowls. Everybody agreed from the start there was no shame in paper plates so long as you bought the best. It was the same every year: should we or shouldn't we, and where to meet, and what to eat, barbecue, or fry, and every year they arranged themselves under the identical beech tree for the reunion, every year the same with allowances for births and deaths. As the years went on the number of aunts and uncles diminished and the number of cousins increased, but there had never yet in this century been a reunion where Uncle Cleveland wasn't prime mover.

So when Elizabeth looked up from chopping the celery for potato salad and saw two bright tips of a man's shoes (the kitchen was partitioned from the dining room by a fiberglass curtain which was drawn now to fend off the glare from the toolshed roof) she cried, "Oh, it's Uncle Cleveland!" and ran to him. And there stood the stranger with the note pad in his raised hand.

"I knocked and knocked," he apologized. "You didn't hear."

"It's the fan. It lumbers." She nudged it back a bit with her bare toes. The machine rumbled on, ineffectual but soothing. "It's not Uncle Cleveland, Mama," she said over her shoulder to May.

May looked up from her lap of green beans and shook her head. "No, it isn't." May didn't say what is a stranger doing in my house and she didn't say welcome either. She just looked.

"The ladies at the store said here was where to find Cleveland Inglish." He held out the crumpled map as proof.

"You're early, that's all." May dumped another load of bean strings onto the newspaper by her chair. "He owe you?" The remarks were getting down to business now.

"I'm writing a feature on Mrs. Harris—life and works and that."

"Uncle Cleveland did used to work for her some," May grudged. "Off and on."

"But she's dead, years and years!" Elizabeth ran her knife over the whetstone and tested the blade on her thumb.

"She wrote about us," May said. "She got some of it wrong." She bent a bean till its back broke. "She meant well, for all the good it does."

"Are you writing a story story or a true story?" Elizabeth kept her eyes on the knife and guided it gravely through the celery stalks. She never imagined that he might be uncomfortable there, in the doorway, waiting for them to produce Cleveland. She did not realize him at all. She finished chopping and laid the blade aside.

"A true story," he told her gently, as though she were a child. It was the way she listened, yearning for some remark she had never heard, some refutation, some proof.

"I can show you her studio," she offered. He set his tea glass down on the sink apart from theirs so if that made a difference they could tell which was which. "Mama?" she asked in afterthought.

"You're old enough to know better," May said. Maybe she was teasing. Maybe she meant the Posted signs.

"It's not life or death," Elizabeth said.

"Shoes!" May exhorted, but she needn't have, for Elizabeth was already tying on her sneakers.

"If Uncle Cleveland comes in before we're back, ring the dinner bell." She was out of the house and away before the fan had a chance to turn back to her.

The writer's name was Paul Montgomery. She stored it up, but never would call him anything other than sir or mister, though there wasn't a decade between them, just the wide world. They went overland, uphill all the way, and summer had its full go with the trail. "You mustn't resist the brambles," she advised, hearing him tearing himself free, his shirt already picked in a dozen places. "Just back out of them." She demonstrated. He got entangled again. "It's no country for a man with a temper," she agreed as he struggled furiously with the blackberry runner slapped across his back. They could hear Uncle Billy's gun, pop-pop-pop. And the crows laughing. Going under a plum thicket her scarf was torn from her hair. They paused while she retied it. The blueberries were long past prime, but she found a handful and shared with him.

"Almost there," she encouraged. "I can smell the verbena." At the summit they stood undismayed before the fierce sign that proclaimed

KEEP OUT

WHO THIS

MEAN YOU.

"Not us," she said. "Not me." She knew a place were the fence was down. They crossed boldly.

He stood with one arm resting on the warm fieldstone wall that belted the household gardens from the fields. Mint and verbena and lavender and geraniums bloomed pungently at his feet. The last irises were gone to parchment now, and the shasta daisies were taking their turn. Hollyhocks towered over the iron gate to the chapel. It was locked. Everything was locked. The place was like an opera set, and needed moonlight for its true majesty. Even the graves, as he could see through the gate, looked cute and common. The stone was baking. An undecided lizard, half green, half brown, darted past at eye level on the wall, its blue throat puffing.

"Must be gone fishing," Elizabeth reported, returning empty-handed from her quest for the keys. "Her workroom's back there. We can look in the windows." She led the way. Her quick eye spotted the lizard. She caught him and let him run up her arm and down her arm and away into the sunstruck flowers. The writer peered in the window at the lifeless studio, left as it had been when the enterprise of thought and imagination ceased, decades since. This was oblivion. The bundled papers were yellowed; he could catch a whiff of them, a cellar dankness. The table stood just so in the slant of light, the ink gone to dust in the well. They moved from pane to pane, staring into obscurity.

"Better it had all burned down than this," she said.

"No." He sounded sure.

"It's like my grandmother: she saved my grand-father's love letters, even after he died; she kept them in a sack under her bed. So we couldn't ever pry, she cut them into quilt scraps. Now she's dead and it's Mama saving them and nobody says so but it makes us sad and ashamed and I'll burn them one day, yes I will!"

"This is different," he assured her at once. It made her think of the man with the camera who had said, "Two separate truths."

"I thought the bell would have rung by now." She stood listening. "If he doesn't come till tomorrow, will you be back?"

"Is he sharp?"

"You mean Uncle Cleveland?" She laughed. "You'll be pressed to keep up."

"He must be ninety."

"That don't differ."

"Why did you think I was your uncle? Do I look so old?"

"You're you. Just yourself. Born in God's time and going to last till you're done." She brushed a crumb of moss from her blouse. "It was your shoes. Being new and all, city shoes."

He looked at his unexceptional feet.

"Old folks never wear out their shoes. Not even the bottoms get scratched much. And the tops never crease. *You* know. And so when I saw them—"

"Well, I never noticed."

"It could break your heart. The same as all these things of hers waiting for her to return." She polished a little twig smooth as a chicken bone and broke it in three. She let it drop.

"Have you read any of her books?"

"After sixteen they caint make you," she said.

They were already halfway down the ridge when the farm bell rang and rang.

"That's Bremen," she reckoned. "God never gave him quittin' sense."

Back at the house she sent him round to the front door like company while she slipped into the kitchen. "Only thing," she said in parting, "Uncle Cleveland's slightly deef." They could hear May and Uncle Billy shouting their welcomes, and the rough monotone of the patriarch's replies.

Uncle Billy told his favorite joke, twice, then went to clean his crow gun. May plumped the pillows behind the old man's granite back and set a glass of tea beside him. Sophie and Bremen, blue jeans damp to the knees from wading in the creek, pressed to the old soul, one on each side of the recliner, showing what they had brought him from the woods, and what had come in the mail, and the oil painting of Paul Lilley's Texas pony the lady had given Elizabeth for a song. The black-and-white cat strolled in through the wide-open door like family and posed at Cleveland's feet, gazing all the way up those blade-thin legs in their white trousers to his vest where the gold chain and Masonic fob rose and fell conversationally. Elizabeth went upstairs and put on the blue dress he had liked the last time, and brushed the tangles from her hair. She announced her coming with each step in her whited shoes from Easter. She curtsied and he called her Priscilla and asked her to sing.

"With or without?"

"Without? What kind of singing is that?"

So she got her flat-top guitar with the little red hearts painted around the sounding hole and she sang as loudly as she could bear to, and he must have heard her. Paul Montgomery did, waiting on the front porch to be remembered.

"Whose red car is that?" Billy was back with a new joke. The kids looked out.

" '76 Charger," Bremen said. There was a silence, then May stepped in.

"Where's your professor?"

And that's when Elizabeth remembered him and asked him in.

"He's writing about Corra Harris, for the Sunday magazine," she explained to the old man.

"Ghosts, ghosts, ghosts," Sophie and Bremen chanted. They once reported having seen a "spectacle" in that tilting barn.

"Behave," May told the kids, but she let them stay. Billy stayed too, just kept butting in, and Elizabeth, who had heard every word at least once before, went to peel potatoes. By suppertime it had been decided that it was no trouble, none at all, and would Mr. Montgomery stay and eat with them?

He would.

The lady writer got herself mentioned time and again, but nothing much came of it that Paul Montgomery saw. He kept his note pad open just in case. He was a city boy all right, speaking of baby cows and 2% milk. Bremen took it on himself to mimic Aunt Lilah's boy Bud, spearing his green beans wrong-handed and nibbling them sideways like a rabbit. He'd been brought up better, you could tell. It was pure devilment. Aunt Lilah and them had that effect, even long distance. (One year's reunion Bud shot out the glass ball on the lightning rod, on the north one, the most important one by the chimney, and all Lilah Inglish Ames would say was, "Well, well," and go on chewing chicken salad.) Sophie thought Montgomery was "weird," having never been that close to a red-haired man with a mustache. "Vinnie vannie veddy veddy lou lou lou," she jeered at him, eating pickles right off his plate without asking. She was seated to his left, and Uncle Cleveland to his right, so that the writer could shout into the better ear. Elizabeth sat around the table from him while she sat at all. She ate in a hurry and excused herself. They could hear the porch swing creaking and her soft voice singing some sad thing, without the guitar.

"Well, she's just full of summer," Horace said at large.

"Summer don't last long, even in a good year," May said. And she wasn't looking at the sky.

When Montgomery left to drive to his motel on the interstate, Sophie and Bremen sprinkled him with goodnights from their windows upstairs. "Have you heard any news?" Sophie called to Bremen, silly with sleep. "Not a word. What have you heard?" he ritually replied. "Welcome back! Come again!" they chorused as the red Dodge drove off. It was too dark to wave. Only Elizabeth knew that he had decided to come back to the reunion with a camera, and questions for the others. It was more than his deadline he was considering when he said, "I need more time."

In the dark Elizabeth sat on the porch and thought about the colt in Paul Lilley's lower field. She walked out in the moonlight down across the meadow where the lady painter had laughed at her scruples. "I brought you apples," she coaxed, but the horse held aloof, snorting, haughty. "Last chance," she warned, but he was coy.

He trembled all over. He trotted deeper into the shadows. "All right." She flung the apples then and ran up the path toward home. The lights were on like a funeral was happening, and those gusts of laughter, and the clatter of pans. She heard the first tentative scratchings of Cleveland's fiddle, and Horace calling her to bring her guitar.

It was just like always. The Inglish population had remained stable during the year so there were no eyes seeking resemblances to the departed and that bittersweet pang when they were discovered. Aunt Goldie was meeker than ever. She sat off to the right of Cleveland's throne, on a kitchen chair; she was neither crumpled nor crisp, just resigned. She had lived a while at the State Hospital when she was younger, had started crying one day at breakfast and couldn't stop; for weeks and weeks she had wept, giving no reasons. When May spoke to her now she looked up, eyes swimming, but had nothing to say. Aunt Lilah and Big Bud drove in about eleven-thirty. Little Bud was going for a three-year pin at Sunday school so they had to hang around home long enough for him to put in his appearance, then they drove directly on. They brought watermelons on chipped ice in a galvanized tub. Lilah's daughter Patty and her groom were already present, joking their newlywed jokes with Uncle Billy. Grant and Tillie and their five drove in not long after the watermelons were set to earth from the back of Big Bud's Buick. And the Bliss sisters arrived, on their canes, with their cushions and scrapbooks. There were more dogs than usual and indistinguishable children seen from time to time dragging first Sophie's Belgian bunny and then Bremen's round and round the springhouse. The elders, in perfect state, arranged themselves by bloodline and years under the beech tree. And all the time there was talk, and renewals, and measurings, and little disputes about what year and just where and wasn't it a Reo and not a Model T? and the tap-tap-tap of May flouring the cake pans and one wife or another running out of the house and setting something on the spread tables and running back in so quick she could almost pass to and fro on one slam of the screen door. The older cousins were stationed along the tables to ward off flies and jaybirds and dogs. Everybody's kind and nobody's kin Johnny Calhoun drove up in his restored Packard after they all had a plateful and a big waxed cup of lemonade and the good hush had fallen where hunger in the open air overcomes sociability. Someone had counted and reckoned there were fifty-four human beings present, or possibly only fifty-three, owing to a confusion about the James twins whose mama, despite psychological advice in *Family Circle,* continued to dress them alike.

"Take out and eat!" they cried to Johnny Calhoun as they'd have cried to anyone venturing into the yard then, friend or foe. But they knew Johnny. He was a chenille manufacturer, forty in a year or so, and wild in the way that made him worth the trouble he caused. He was the best-looking one there for his type, fair and fiery, like Uncle Cleveland when he was a stripling. But Uncle Cleveland had married young and for all time, and Johnny was still free. Mighty free, some said. Patty ran up to him and kissed him right on the mouth and he made faces over her shoulder, brows high and delighted, then winked at Jeff, whose responsibility she was now. Who didn't laugh didn't see. Aunt Goldie eased on up to the house to take her snuff in private. Folks expanded with lunch and love and the elders in their circle nodded and woke and nodded and spoke. If they noticed how Paul Montgomery was watching everything shrewder than a cousin-in-law, they just guessed he was Elizabeth's beau and made him welcome. Welcome all.

It was the custom for Uncle Cleveland as senior to pray over the food before they ate it and the other brothers and sisters of his generation to pray afterward. Uncle Tatum began it now, standing upright, four-square, hand on lapel, eyes shut tight against the distractions of the younguns tearing back and forth like hellions. Elizabeth stood at the outer ring of the connection, near the childish freedom of the lawn where cartwheels and somersets were underway. It was her wish to escape now, before the music-making. Once they called on her she couldn't say no, not to family. She studied her locked fingers, head down, not to mimic piety but rather to avoid the too-plucking gaze of the aunts. "I'll never love but one man!" they'd all heard her say since she was a babe, and they kept watch to see if she had made a fool of herself yet. Uncle Tatum said, "Amen," and Aunt Goldie stood, shyly, for her own prayer, lost among picnic debris and her own rollicking pinafore collar.

"Oh God," Goldie quavered, and her tears, never far off, began to fall. This was the saddest part of the day, they all feared for her so. "Goldie's next," they thought, and gazed and gazed, memorizing every living detail. Elizabeth slipped farther away, till she could hear no childish voices, no ancient piety, and no music at all. The gray tabby from the hilltop farm crept past her in the long grass.

Elizabeth lay back on the warm earth and sang so lightly that the kinglets and phoebes resting in the bower went undisturbed. She moved her head to the left until the elm shadow lay cool on her eyes. She watched a great satiny fool of an ant, clown-striped,

race headlong off a blackberry vine above her. The sun
outlined everything in silver. The grass looked like cellophane. And there wasn't a breeze in all the world to
turn a leaf.

There was something else about Johnny Calhoun: he
was quiet as a cat. He nudged her with the toe of his shoe.
"Look what I found," he said, as he said every summer to
some girl, to Patty, to all of them, that Johnny Calhoun.
She stood up too quickly. It took a moment for the
landscape to settle in her thoughts. She stamped her
tingling foot, dazzled. She could talk and talk among kin,
overheard. Now she couldn't even say boo.

"They were calling for you," he reported. He had
stripped off his tie long since; it trailed from his coat
pocket. There was razor burn on his throat, below his
ear. He eased his collar with one finger.

She shook her head, denying all claims. She dusted
her fingers on her skirt. "Lilah can play as pretty a bass
run as they'll hear, or need to."

He turned her hand palm up and set a little present
on it. "For Christmas or the Fourth of July," he said.

"Oh I caint. I mustn't. I don't have anything for
you." It was not so heavy; it was not very large.

"It's yours," he said. "It's for you."

"I caint think," she said. "What do you suppose it is!"
She unwrapped it a tag at a time, not to tease him but
herself. When she got the ribbon unknotted, she coiled
it tidy as a clerk and filed it in his pocket. "Well I don't
know," she murmured, filled with exquisite dread. She
drew the paper off. A music box gleamed on her up-
turned palm. It might have been the most precious
egg. It took her breath in surmise.

"I'm listening," she said cautiously. He pressed the
switch and the melody dripped out, three dozen notes
of a nocturne.

"Chopin," he told her.

When it ran down he wound it again.

"Johnny?" she wondered, more to herself than not. Calhoun lit his cigarette and imperceptibly waited. One old leaf on the tulip tree was stricken with palsy. It shook and shook. It might have been any ordinary day since Eden fell. She never did see the hawk, circling the sun. When she looked at it again, the tulip tree was motionless, every leaf in place.

"Johnny," she decided.

The music was over, and the melons devoured, and yellow jackets had come and drunk from the rinds. One of the twins had been stung so the other had to try it. Sympathy swirled back and forth between them as everyone gave advice. Most of the food had been cleared away and the white sheets that covered the plank tables had to be weighted with stones. In the winding-down part of the day everyone got more related somehow, and Paul Montgomery, feeling shut out, shut his notebook for good. He locked his briefcase in the car, then realized that was too citified a thing to do: heads had turned at the rasping of his key in the car door, indicting him, and so he left his trappings lying frankly on the back seat, the windows down, his suit coat on the front seat with the garnered facts in the black book jutting from the pocket just the way Uncle Cleveland's Prince Albert showed, like a handkerchief, in its red can. Montgomery swung his camera around his neck and set off up the hill to the studio for some pictures. He knew his way well enough, but he looked around for Elizabeth, hoping she might come along. She had disappeared earlier and despite several alarms had failed to show. One of the dogs heaved himself to his feet and volunteered for the hike. They set out in

the best of spirits. There were massing clouds that
would make his camera work more challenging.

He finished the roll of film and, seeing the dogs
panting in the shade of the tainted well, he crossed to
the spigot at the house and let the animal drink from
his cupped hands. He thought he heard the television
playing inside; he hallooed and knocked, but no one
answered. He paused one last time at the chapel gate
and peered through at the graves. Already the first
tentative sentences of his article were forming in his
thoughts. He turned back down the ridge toward the
Inglish farm. The dog suddenly took an interest in
something just beyond his view, barked and looked
away and did not bark again.

Johnny Calhoun was sitting with his back to a tree,
not smoking, not smiling, not speaking. He shook his
head to warn Montgomery not to step on Elizabeth's
outflung hand still clasping the music box. She lay
sleeping, an arm across her eyes to ward off the sun.

Johnny brushed a ladybug from his ear. "We'll be
along," he told the writer, neither unnerved nor ami-
able. Montgomery jogged on past, the camera beating
against his pounding heart.

He left without making the entire rounds of all the
guests, though he did press the stiff warm hands of the
Bliss sisters; he congratulated May on her dinner and
nodded to Horace's raised hat, but Uncle Cleveland
was asleep again and Goldie was distant.

"Let us hear," someone cried after him from the
porch. Uncle Billy already had his chair tipped back
against the bee-stuffed post and dozed malevolently. It
was Lilah's newlywed Patty who noticed Elizabeth and
Johnny Calhoun were both still unaccounted for and
when the black-and-white tomcat leaped onto her familiar lap she slapped it away with a remark that made

her groom look sharp and Uncle Billy, that impostor, laugh.

The number of tourists driving by and asking after the lady writer's remains increased dramatically in the weeks after Montgomery's article came out. Uncle Billy got so aggravated with the interruptions that he began taking his chair out on the back porch, leaving Horace to direct traffic. Not every Sunday would a literary pilgrim find Elizabeth Inglish on the porch, guitar in hand, waiting for the evening train to pass through Paul Lilley's meadow, but when she was there she stared coolly past the stranger, mute, head held high, as though nothing whether trivial or profound would distract her from her reverie. Some thought she was blind, and walked back to their car to mention it to the others. And some had the impression she was a fool.

How Far She Went

They had quarreled all morning, squalled all summer about the incidentals: how tight the girl's cut-off jeans were, the "Every Inch a Woman" T-shirt, her choice of music and how loud she played it, her practiced inattention, her sullen look. Her granny wrung out the last boiled dishcloth, pinched it to the line, giving the basin a sling and a slap, the water flying out in a scalding arc onto the Queen Anne's lace by the path, never mind if it bloomed, that didn't make it worth anything except to chiggers, but the girl would cut it by the everlasting armload and cherish it in the old churn, going to that much trouble for a weed but not bending once—unbegged—to pick the nearest bean; she was sulking now. Bored. Displaced.

"And what do you think happens to a chigger if nobody ever walks by his weed?" her granny asked, heading for the house with that sidelong uneager unanswered glance, hoping for what? The surprise gift of a smile? Nothing. The woman shook her head and said it. "Nothing." The door slammed behind her. Let it.

"I hate it here!" the girl yelled then. She picked up a stick and broke it and threw the pieces—one from each hand—at the laundry drying in the noon. Missed. Missed.

Then she turned on her bare, haughty heel and set off high-shouldered into the heat, quick but not far, not far enough—no road was *that* long—only as far as she dared. At the gate, a rusty chain swinging between two lichened posts, she stopped, then backed up the raw drive to make a run at the barrier, lofting, clearing it clean, her long hair wild in the sun. Triumphant, she looked back at the house where she caught at the dark window her granny's face in its perpetual eclipse of disappointment, old at fifty. She stepped back, but the girl saw her.

"You don't know me!" the girl shouted, chin high, and ran till her ribs ached.

As she rested in the rattling shade of the willows, the little dog found her. He could be counted on. He barked all the way, and squealed when she pulled the burr from his ear. They started back to the house for lunch. By then the mailman had long come and gone in the old ruts, leaving the one letter folded now to fit the woman's apron pocket.

If bad news darkened her granny's face, the girl ignored it. Didn't talk at all, another of her distancings, her defiances. So it was as they ate that the woman summarized, "Your daddy wants you to cash in the plane ticket and buy you something. School clothes. For here."

Pale, the girl stared, defenseless only an instant before blurting out, "You're lying."

The woman had to stretch across the table to leave her handprint on that blank cheek. She said, not caring if it stung or not, "He's been planning it since he sent you here."

"I could turn this whole house over, dump it! Leave you slobbering over that stinking jealous dog in the dust!" The girl trembled with the vision, with the strength it gave her. It made her laugh. "Scatter the Holy Bible like confetti and ravel the crochet into miles of stupid string! I could! I will! I won't stay here!" But she didn't move, not until her tears rose to meet her color, and then to escape the shame of minding so much she fled. Just headed away, blind. It didn't matter, this time, how far she went.

The woman set her thoughts against fretting over their bickering, just went on unalarmed with chores, clearing off after the uneaten meal, bringing in the laundry, scattering corn for the chickens, ladling manure tea onto the porch flowers. She listened though. She always had been a listener. It gave her a cocked look. She forgot why she had gone into the girl's empty room, that ungirlish, tenuous lodging place with its bleak order, its ready suitcases never unpacked, the narrow bed, the contested radio on the windowsill. The woman drew the cracked shade down between the radio and the August sun. There wasn't anything else to do.

It was after six when she tied on her rough oxfords and walked down the drive and dropped the gate chain and headed back to the creosoted shed where she kept her tools. She took a hoe for snakes, a rake, shears to trim the grass where it grew, and seed in her pocket to scatter where it never had grown at all. She put the tools and her gloves and the bucket in the trunk of the old Chevy, its prime and rust like an Appaloosa's spots through the chalky white finish. She left the trunk open and the tool handles sticking out. She wasn't going far.

The heat of the day had broken, but the air was thick, sultry, weighted with honeysuckle in second bloom and the Nu-Grape scent of kudzu. The maple and poplar leaves turned over, quaking, silver. There wouldn't be any rain. She told the dog to stay, but he knew a trick. He stowed away when she turned her back, leaped right into the trunk with the tools, then gave himself away with exultant barks. Hearing him, her court jester, she stopped the car and welcomed him into the front seat beside her. Then they went on. Not a mile from her gate she turned onto the blue gravel of the cemetery lane, hauled the gearshift into reverse to whoa them, and got out to take the idle walk down to her buried hopes, bending all along to rout out a handful of weeds from between the markers of old acquaintance. She stood there and read, slow. The dog whined at her hem; she picked him up and rested her chin on his head, then he wriggled and whined to run free, contrary and restless as a child.

The crows called strong and bold MOM! MOM! A trick of the ear to hear it like that. She knew it was the crows, but still she looked around. No one called her that now. She was done with that. And what was it worth anyway? It all came to this: solitary weeding. The sinful fumble of flesh, the fear, the listening for a return that never came, the shamed waiting, the un- answered prayers, the perjury on the certificate— hadn't she lain there weary of the whole lie and it only beginning? and a voice telling her, "Here's your baby, here's your girl," and the swaddled package meaning no more to her than an extra anything, something store-bought, something she could take back for a refund.

"Tie her to the fence and give her a bale of hay," she had murmured, drugged, and they teased her, excused her for such a welcoming, blaming the anesthesia, but it went deeper than that; *she* knew, and the *baby* knew:

there was no love in the begetting. That was the secret, unforgivable, that not another good thing could ever make up for, where all the bad had come from, like a visitation, a punishment. She knew that was why Sylvie had been wild, had gone to earth so early, and before dying had made this child in sudden wedlock, a child who would be just like her, would carry the hurting on into another generation. A matter of time. No use raising her hand. But she *had* raised her hand. Still wore on its palm the memory of the sting of the collision with the girl's cheek; had she broken her jaw? Her heart? Of course not. She said it aloud: "Takes more than that."

She went to work then, doing what she could with her old tools. She pecked the clay on Sylvie's grave, new-looking, unhealed after years. She tried again, scattering seeds from her pocket, every last possible one of them. Off in the west she could hear the pulp-wood cutters sawing through another acre across the lake. Nearer, there was the racket of motorcycles laboring cross-country, insect-like, distracting.

She took her bucket to the well and hung it on the pump. She had half filled it when the bikers roared up, right down the blue gravel, straight at her. She let the bucket overflow, staring. On the back of one of the machines was the girl. Sylvie's girl! Her bare arms wrapped around the shirtless man riding between her thighs. They were first. The second biker rode alone. She studied their strangers' faces as they circled her. They were the enemy, all of them. Laughing. The girl was laughing too, laughing like her mama did. Out in the middle of nowhere the girl had found these two men, some moth-musk about her drawing them (too soon!) to what? She shouted it: "What in God's—" They roared off without answering her, and the bucket of water tipped over, spilling its stain blood-dark on the red dust.

The dog went wild barking, leaping after them, snapping at the tires, and there was no calling him down. The bikers made a wide circuit of the church-yard, then roared straight across the graves, leaping the ditch and landing upright on the road again, head-ing off toward the reservoir.

Furious, she ran to her car, past the barking dog, this time leaving him behind, driving after them, horn blowing nonstop, to get back what was not theirs. She drove after them knowing what they did not know, that all the roads beyond that point dead-ended. She surprised them, swinging the Impala across their path, cutting them off; let them hit it! They stopped. She got out, breathing hard, and said, when she could, "She's underage." Just that. And put out her claiming hand with an authority that made the girl's arms drop from the man's insolent waist and her legs tremble.

"I was just riding," the girl said, not looking up.

Behind them the sun was heading on toward down. The long shadows of the pines drifted back and forth in the same breeze that puffed the distant sails on the lake. Dead limbs creaked and clashed overhead like the antlers of locked and furious beasts.

"Sheeeut," the lone rider said. "I told you." He braced with his muddy boot and leaned out from his machine to spit. The man the girl had been riding with had the invading sort of eyes the woman had spent her lifetime bolting doors against. She met him now, face to face.

"Right there, missy," her granny said, pointing be-hind her to the car.

The girl slid off the motorcycle and stood halfway between her choices. She started slightly at the poosh!

as he popped another top and chugged the beer in one uptilting of his head. His eyes never left the woman's. When he was through, he tossed the can high, flipping it end over end. Before it hit the ground he had his pistol out and, firing once, winged it into the lake.

"Freaking lucky shot," the other one grudged.

"I don't need luck," he said. He sighted down the barrel of the gun at the woman's head. "POW!" he yelled, and when she recoiled, he laughed. He swung around to the girl; he kept aiming the gun, here, there, high, low, all around. "Y'all settle it," he said, with a shrug.

The girl had to understand him then, had to know him, had to know better. But still she hesitated. He kept looking at her, then away.

"She's fifteen," her granny said. "You can go to jail."

"You can go to hell," he said.

"Probably will," her granny told him. "I'll save you a seat by the fire." She took the girl by the arm and drew her to the car; she backed up, swung around, and headed out the road toward the churchyard for her tools and dog. The whole way the girl said nothing, just hunched against the far door, staring hard-eyed out at the pines going past.

The woman finished watering the seed in, and collected her tools. As she worked, she muttered, "It's your own kin buried here, you might have the decency to glance this way one time . . ." The girl was finger-tweezing her eyebrows in the side mirror. She didn't look around as the dog and the woman got in. Her granny shifted hard, sending the tools clattering in the trunk.

When they came to the main road, there were the men. Watching for them. Waiting for them. They kicked their machines into life and followed, close, bumping them, slapping the old fenders, yelling. The girl gave a wild glance around at the one by her door and said, "Gran'ma?" and as he drew his pistol, "Gran'ma!" just as the gun nosed into the open window. She frantically cranked the glass up between her and the weapon, and her granny, seeing, spat, "Fool!" She never had been one to pray for peace or rain. She stamped the accelerator right to the floor.

The motorcycles caught up. Now she braked, hard, and swerved off the road into an alley between the pines, not even wide enough for the school bus, just a fire scrape that came out a quarter mile from her own house, if she could get that far. She slewed on the pine straw, then righted, tearing along the dark tunnel through the woods. She had for the time being bested them; they were left behind. She was winning. Then she hit the wallow where the tadpoles were already five weeks old. The Chevy plowed in and stalled. When she got it cranked again, they were stuck. The tires spattered mud three feet up the near trunks as she tried to spin them out, to rock them out. Useless. "Get out and run!" she cried, but the trees were too close on the passenger side. The girl couldn't open her door. She wasted precious time having to crawl out under the steering wheel. The woman waited but the dog ran on.

They struggled through the dusky woods, their pace slowed by the thick straw and vines. Overhead, in the last light, the martins were reeling free and sure after their prey.

"Why? Why?" the girl gasped, as they lunged down the old deer trail. Behind them they could hear shots, and glass breaking as the men came to the bogged car. The woman kept on running, swatting their way clear through the shoulder-high weeds. They could see the Greer cottage, and made for it. But it was ivied-over, padlocked, the woodpile dry-rotting under its tarp, the electric meterbox empty on the pole. No help there.

The dog, excited, trotted on, yelping, his lips white-flecked. He scented the lake and headed that way, urging them on with thirsty yips. On the clay shore, treeless, deserted, at the utter limit of land, they stood defenseless, listening to the men coming on, between them and home. The woman pressed her hands to her mouth, stifling her cough. She was exhausted. She couldn't think.

"We can get under!" the girl cried suddenly, and pointed toward the Greers' dock, gap-planked, its walkway grounded on the mud. They splashed out to it, wading in, the woman grabbing up the telltale, tattletale dog in her arms. They waded out to the far end and ducked under. There was room between the foam floats for them to crouch neck-deep.

The dog wouldn't hush, even then; never had yet, and there wasn't time to teach him. When the woman realized that, she did what she had to do. She grabbed him whimpering; held him; held him under till the struggle ceased and the bubbles rose silver from his fur. They crouched there then, the two of them, submerged to the shoulders, feet unsteady on the slimed lake bed. They listened. The sky went from rose to ocher to violet in the cracks over their heads. The motorcycles had stopped now. In the silence there was the glissando of locusts, the dry crunch of boots on the flinty beach, their low man-talk drifting as they prowled back and forth. One of them struck a match.

"—they in these woods we could burn 'em out."

The wind carried their voices away into the pines. Some few words eddied back.

"—lippy old smartass do a little work on her knees besides praying—"

Laughter. It echoed off the deserted house. They were getting closer.

One of them strode directly out to the dock, walked on the planks over their heads. They could look up and see his boot soles. He was the one with the gun. He slapped a mosquito on his bare back and cursed. The carp, roused by the troubling of the waters, came nosing around the dock, guzzling and snorting. The girl and her granny held still, so still. The man fired his pistol into the shadows, and a wounded fish thrashed, dying. The man knelt and reached for it, chuffing out his beery breath. He belched. He pawed the lake for the dead fish, cursing as it floated out of reach. He shot it again, firing at it till it sank and the gun was empty. Cursed that too. He stood then and unzipped and relieved himself of some of the beer. They had to listen to that. To know that about him. To endure that, unprotesting.

Back and forth on shore the other one ranged, restless. He lit another cigarette. He coughed. He called, "Hey! They got away, man, that's all. Don't get your shorts in a wad. Let's go."

"Yeah." He finished. He zipped. He stumped back across the planks and leaped to shore, leaving the dock tilting amid widening ripples. Underneath, they waited.

The bike cranked. The other ratcheted, ratcheted, then coughed, caught, roared. They circled, cut deep ruts, slung gravel, and went. Their roaring died away and away. Crickets resumed and a near frog bic-bic-bicked.

Under the dock, they waited a little longer to be sure. Then they ducked below the water, scraped out from under the pontoon, and came up into free air, slogging toward shore. It had seemed warm enough in the water. Now they shivered. It was almost night. One streak of light still stood reflected on the darkening lake, drew itself thinner, narrowing into a final cancellation of day. A plane winked its way west.

The girl was trembling. She ran her hands down her arms and legs, shedding water like a garment. She sighed, almost a sob. The woman held the dog in her arms; she dropped to her knees upon the random stones and murmured, private, haggard, "Oh, honey," three times, maybe all three times for the dog, maybe once for each of them. The girl waited, watching. Her granny rocked the dog like a baby, like a dead child, rocked slower and slower and was still.

"I'm sorry," the girl said then, avoiding the dog's inert, empty eye.

"It was him or you," her granny said, finally, looking up. Looking her over. "Did they mess with you? With your britches? Did they?"

"No!" Then, quieter, "No, ma'am."

When the woman tried to stand up she staggered, lightheaded, clumsy with the freight of the dog. "No, ma'am," she echoed, fending off the girl's "Let me." And she said again, "It was him or you. I know that. I'm not going to rub your face in it." They saw each other as well as they could in that failing light, in any light.

The woman started toward home, saying, "Around here, we bear our own burdens." She led the way along the weedy shortcuts. The twilight bleached the dead limbs of the pines to bone. Insects sang in the thickets, silencing at their oncoming.

"We'll see about the car in the morning," the woman said. She bore her armful toward her own moth-ridden dusk-to-dawn security light with that country grace she had always had when the earth was reliably progressing underfoot. The girl walked close behind her, exactly where *she* walked, matching her pace, matching her stride, close enough to put her hand forth (if the need arose) and touch her granny's back where the faded voile was clinging damp, the merest gauze between their wounds.

Doing This, Saying That, to Applause

"*He keeps to himself. No one in this department knows him except superficially.*"

The green paint, that lurid park-bench color, is beginning to blister and peel from the door. The oxidized screens weep rust onto the cement block walls. His key turns with its characteristic hitch. The door falls open, thumping into a dinette chair. He goes inside quickly, his footsteps soundless on the threadbare, gritty carpet. He closes the door behind him. It locks automatically. This has been a fashionable address.

"*He keeps up a wall, a very friendly wall.*"

The windows, sealed with paint and grime, have not opened in years. The drapes have faded, sunspotted, dappled with age. The venetian blinds, hung in hope of modernity, have yellowed like time-stained teeth. Neither drapes nor blinds have been opened more or less than they are now for years, the same day and night as though the windows and the world beyond are a painting. The bed has not been made. The covers lie twisted, tangled, wrack at ebb tide. The rancid pillow still bears the impress of his head.

"*He is a responsible human being.*"

He fetches forth the contents of his many pockets:

pens, pads, address book, wallet, change, keys. There
are a great many keys, a lifetime of keys; they settle
with a chime onto the stamped-metal ashtray. He will
not chip any more paint from the derelict dresser, gray
imitation oak with a dingy mirror around whose frame
snapshots yellow and curl. On a step table of the same
false wood, the phone and its directory rest askew.

"He is conscientious, punctual. This is incredible."
In the long walk-in closet, dank as a cellar, shelved
ceiling to floor, are a variety of mementos hidden mod-
estly away: trophies for scholarship and civic activity, a
scrapbook of himself, younger, collegiate, doing this,
saying that, to applause. Along the floor, beneath his
treed shoes, are bundles of old university periodicals
from which he has not yet deleted his triumphant self,
unsent extra copies for family and friends. He has not
followed through. He has hoarded his early triumph.
He grapples his crumpled suit onto a hanger, peel-
ing the trousers off over his shoes. He goes back into
the main room of the efficiency and sits in the vinyl
chair to untie his shoes. His feet are hot, as though he
has been wading in hell.

"I wish you could just say he was wacky and let that be it."
In his sock feet, in his boxer shorts and T-shirt, he
sits reading the accumulated mail: circulars, charity ap-
peals, news magazines, the bills for his auto insurance.
In another year the car will be paid for. He opens a
box of cereal and prepares a bowl. He eats while he
reads. The milk that spills on the floor he wipes with
the heel of his sock.

*"He has always been such a gentleman, a perfectionist about
his reports, well-disciplined, mild-mannered, punctual as the
stars."*

As evening closes in, the walls exude a basement chill. He flicks on the ceiling light in the kitchenette and from under the sink retrieves a can of insecticide. The empty cabinets are lined with seven-year-old news; there are no dishes, no foodstuffs, nothing. Everything edible is stored within the dinky refrigerator. A drainer of dishes stands in the rusty sink.

He slumps on the bedside, the blue light of the television washing him in its eerie glow. From time to time he sprays at bold waterbugs with the aerosol death-stream. The room reeks of petroleum distillates and burnt coffee. The phone rings. He does not stir, except to lower the volume on the television.

"He has hurt no one but himself."

On the eleven o'clock news he hears himself reported missing. He starts up from the bed in refreshed terror. Let me be! he longs to shout. Keep out of it, keep out. It is only a matter of time before all of it comes to light.

"When this happens to someone you know, you just can't explain it. This finishes his career."

He has hanged himself in his vices, in his habits.

"When I read how they found a body in the trunk of that stolen car I thought oh goodness if that's our colleague! Of course it wasn't."

He paces back and forth over the wretched carpet. He makes a decision. He twitches on the string that swings from the bare bulb in the closet. The sudden light glares on the miserable archives, the tarnished trophies, the scrapbooks, the dusty shoes. He drags out a suitcase and carries it into the other room.

"If he is framed, why run away?"

and begins stuffing it with clothing. Realizing it is
mad to flee infamy defended only by a suitcase of clean
underwear, he begins to laugh, bends double, and
tears roll down his face, splashing on the dusty floor.

*" 'I am done crying,' says suspect's mother, refusing further
comment."*

In the end he takes nothing at all, only the empty
valise. The apartment, with its mysteries and para-
doxes intact, is locked finally against the prying world.

*"No one answers the phone or the door. His late-model car is
missing."*

He drives all night, dashing from town to town as
children flee, tree to tree, in their twilight searching.

"Whatever he has done, he has done of his own volition."

He stops at a roadside café, buying a gingerbread
man, eating it, buying another, snapping the legs off,
dunking, devouring, next the arms, next the head. He
returns to his car. Day is pinking the eastern horizon.
He sits another hour, digesting, congealing in the chill,
reasoning, probing his circumstances. There are no
conclusions to be reached. He drives out of the parking
lot fast, kicking up gravel that spatters against parked
trucks, dark gas pumps, against the windows of the
café itself. One pebble pings a hole as a bullet might,
leaving a cloudy eye in the flyspecked face of the midnight oasis. It is his only public impropriety. The haggard waitress looks up, curses him, and goes on collect-
ing crockery from the tilting tables.

He travels fast, mindlessly, his suitcase in the trunk
of the car shifting, bounding, bumping with the vio-
lence of his retreat. Mid-morning he roars through an

eye-blink of a town whose lone officer takes umbrage, pursues, apprehends.

"There are two things that trouble me. First, how many times do these things go unreported, for fear, for shame?"

"Just who do you think you are, buddy?" The officer turns aside to spit. "We got laws, you know. Even here."

"And second, how can you tell which is the type to be found hanging by his shirt in his cell?"

"Dear," he begins, on the piece of paper the trusty gives him when he requests it. But the rest of the page, like the suitcase, remains empty.

Manly Conclusions

His wife, Valjean, admitted that Carpenter Petty had a tree-topping temper, but he was slow to lose it; that was in his favor. Still, he had a long memory, and that way of saving things up, until by process of accumulation he had enough evidence to convict. "I don't get mad, I get even," his bumper sticker vaunted. Fair warning. When he was angry he burned like frost, not flame.

Now Valjean stood on the trodden path in the year's first growth of grass, her tablecloth in her arms, and acknowledged an undercurrent in her husband, spoke of it to the greening forsythia with its yellow flowers rain-fallen beneath it, confided it to God and nature. Let God and nature judge. A crow passed between her and the sun, dragging its slow shadow. She glanced up. On Carpenter's behalf she said, "He's always been intense. It wasn't just the war. If you're born a certain way, where's the mending?"

She shook the tablecloth free of the crumbs of breakfast and pinned it to the line. Carpenter liked her biscuits—praised them to all their acquaintances—as well as her old-fashioned willingness to rise before good day and bake for him. Sometimes he woke early too; then he would join her in the kitchen. They would visit as she worked the shortening into the flour, left-handed (as was her mother, whose recipe it was), and pinch off the rounds, laying them as gently in the blackened pan as though she were laying a baby down for its nap. The dough was very quick, very tender. It took a light hand. Valjean knew the value of a light hand.

This morning Carpenter had slept late, beyond his time, and catching up he ate in a rush, his hair damp from the shower, his shirt unbuttoned. He raised neither his eyes nor his voice to praise or complain.

"You'll be better at telling Dennis than I would," he said, finally, leaving it to her.

She had known' for a long time that there was more to loving a man than marrying him, and more to marriage than love. When they were newly wed, there had been that sudden quarrel, quick and furious as a summer squall, between Carpenter and a neighbor over the property line. A vivid memory and a lesson—the two men silhouetted against the setting sun, defending the territory and honor of rental property. Valjean stood by his side, silent, sensing even then that to speak out, to beg, to order, to quake would be to shame him. Nor would it avail. Better to shout "Stay!" to Niagara. Prayer and prevention was the course she decided on, learning how to laugh things off, to make jokes and diversions. If a car cut ahead of them in the parking lot and took the space he had been headed for, before Carpenter could get his window down to berate women drivers, Valjean would say, "I can see why she's in a hurry, just look at her!" as the offender trotted determinedly up the sidewalk and into a beauty salon.

She was subtle enough most times, but maybe he caught on after a while. At any rate, his emotional weather began to moderate. Folks said he had changed, and not for the worse. They gave proper credit to his wife, but the war had a hand in it too. When he got back, most of what he thought and felt had gone underground, and it was his quietness and shrewd good nature that you noticed now. Valjean kept on praying and preventing.

But there are some things you can't prevent, and he had left it to Valjean to break the news to Dennis. Dennis so much like Carpenter that the two of them turned heads in town, father and son, spirit and image. People seemed proud of them from afar as though their striking resemblance reflected credit on all mankind, affirming faith in the continuity of generations. He was like his mama, too, the best of both of them, and try as she might she couldn't find the words to tell him that his dog was dead, to send him off to school with a broken heart. The school bus came early, and in the last-minute flurry of gathering books and lunch money, his poster on medieval armor and his windbreaker, she chose to let the news wait.

She had the whole day then, after he was gone, to find the best words. Musing, she sat on the top step and began cleaning Carpenter's boots—not that he had left them for her to do; he had just left them. She scrubbed and gouged and sluiced away the sticky mud, dipping her rag in a rain puddle. After a moment's deliberation she rinsed the cloth in Lady's water dish. Lady would not mind now; she was beyond thirst. It was burying her that had got Carpenter's boots so muddy.

"Dead," Valjean murmured. For a moment she was overcome, disoriented as one is the instant after cataclysm, while there is yet room for disbelief, before the eyes admit the evidence into the heart. The rag dripped muddy water dark as blood onto the grass.

They had found Lady halfway between the toolshed and the back porch, as near home as she had been able to drag herself. The fine old collie lay dying in their torchlight, bewildered, astonished, trusting them to heal her, to cancel whatever evil this was that had befallen.

Carpenter knelt to investigate. "She's been shot." The meaning of the words and their reverberations brought Valjean to her knees. No way to laugh this off.

"It would have been an accident," she reasoned.

Carpenter gave the road a despairing glance. "If it could have stayed the way it was when we first bought out here . . . you don't keep a dog like this on a chain!"

It had been wonderful those early years, before the developers came with their transits and plat-books and plans for summer cottages in the uplands. The deer had lingered a year or so longer, then had fled across the lake with the moon on their backs. The fields of wild blueberries were fenced off now; what the road-scrapers missed, wildfire got. Lawn crept from acre to acre like a plague. What trees were spared sprouted POSTED and KEEP and TRESPASSERS WILL BE signs. Gone were the tangles of briar and drifted meadow beauty, seedbox and primrose. The ferns retreated yearly deeper into the ravines.

"Goddam weekenders," Carpenter said.

They had lodged official complaint the day three bikers roared through the back lot, scattering the hens, tearing down five lines of wash, and leaving a gap through the grape arbor. The Law came out and made bootless inquiry, stirring things up a little more. The next morning Valjean found their garbage cans overturned. Toilet tissue wrapped every tree in the orchard, a dead rat floated in the well, and their mail-box was battered to earth—that sort of mischief. Wild kids. "Let the Law handle it," Valjean suggested, white-lipped.

"They can do their job and I'll do mine," Carpenter told her. So that time Valjean prayed that the Law would be fast and Carpenter slow, and that was how it went. A deputy came out the next day with a carload of joyriders he had run to earth. "Now I think the worst thing that could happen," the deputy drawled, "is to call their folks, whattya say?" So it had been resolved that way, with reparations paid, and handshakes. That had been several years back; things had settled down some now. Of late there were only the litter and loudness associated with careless vacationers. No lingering hard feelings. In the market, when Valjean met a neighbor's wife, they found pleasant things to speak about; the awkwardness was past. In time they might be friends.

"An accident," Valjean had asserted, her voice odd to her own ears. As though she were surfacing from a deep dive. Around them night was closing in. She shivered. It took her entire will to keep from glancing over her shoulder into the tanglewood through which Lady had plunged, wounded, to reach home.

"Bleeding like this she must have laid a plain track." Carpenter paced the yard, probing at spots with the dimming light of the lantern. He tapped it against his thigh to encourage the weak batteries.

"She's been gone all afternoon," Valjean said. "She could have come miles."

"Not hurt this bad," Carpenter said.

"What are you saying? No. No!" She forced confidence into her voice. "No one around here would do something like this." Fear for him stung her hands and feet like frost. She stood for peace. She stood too suddenly; dizzy, she put out her hand to steady herself. He could feel her trembling.

"It could have been an accident, yeah, like you say." He spoke quietly for her sake. He had learned to do that.

"You see?" she said, her heart lifting a little.

"Yeah." Kneeling again, he shook his head over the dog's labored breathing. "Too bad, old girl; they've done for you."

When the amber light failed from Lady's eyes, Valjean said, breathless, "She was probably trespassing," thinking of all those signs, neon-vivid, warning. He always teased her that she could make excuses for the devil.

"Dogs can't read," he pointed out. "She lived all her life here, eleven, twelve years . . . and she knew this place by heart, every rabbit run, toad hole, and squirrel knot. She was better at weather than the almanac, and there was never a thing she feared except losing us. She kept watch on Dennis like he was her own pup."

"I know . . ." She struggled to choke back the grief. It stuck like a pine cone in her throat. But she wouldn't let it be *her* tears that watered the ground and made the seed of vengeance sprout. For all their sakes she kept her nerve . . .

"And whoever shot her," Carpenter was saying, "can't tell the difference in broad day between ragweed and rainbow. Goddam weekenders!"

They wrapped the dog in Dennis' cradle quilt and set about making a grave. Twilight seeped away into night. The shovel struck fire from the rocks as Carpenter dug. Dennis was at Scout meeting; they wanted to be done before he got home. "There's nothing deader than a dead dog," Carpenter reasoned. "The boy doesn't need to remember her that way."

In their haste, in their weariness, Carpenter shed his

boots on the back stoop and left the shovel leaning against the wall. The wind rose in the night and blew the shovel handle along the shingles with a dry-bones rattle. Waking, alarmed, Valjean put out her hand: Carpenter was there.

Now Valjean resumed work on the boots, concentrating on the task at hand. She cleaned carefully, as though diligence would perfect not only the leather but Carpenter also, cleaning away the mire, anything that might make him lose his balance. From habit, she set the shoes atop the well-house to dry, out of reach of the dog. Then she realized Lady was gone. All her held-back tears came now; she mourned as for a child.

She told Dennis that afternoon. He walked all around the grave, disbelieving. No tears, too old for that; silent, like his father. He gathered straw to lay on the raw earth to keep it from washing. Finally he buried his head in Valjean's shoulder and groaned, "Why?" Hearing that, Valjean thanked God, for hadn't Carpenter asked *Who?* and not *Why?*—as though he had some plan, eye for eye, and needed only to discover upon whom to visit it? Dennis must not learn those ways, Valjean prayed; let my son be in some ways like me . . .

At supper Carpenter waited till she brought dessert before he asked, "Did you tell him?"

Dennis laid down his fork to speak for himself. "I know."

Carpenter beheld his son. "She was shot twice. Once point-blank. Once as she tried to get away."

Valjean's cup wrecked against her saucer. He hadn't told her that! He had held that back, steeping the bitter truth from it all day to serve to the boy. There was no possible antidote. It sank in, like slow poison.

"It's going to be all right," she murmured automatically, her peace of mind spinning away like a chip in a strong current. Her eyes sightlessly explored the sampler on the opposite wall whose motto she had worked during the long winter when she sat at her mother's deathbed: Perfect Love Casts Out Fear.

"You mean Lady knew them? Trusted them? Then they shot her?" Dennis spoke eagerly, proud of his ability to draw manly conclusions. Valjean watched as the boy realized what he was saying. "It's someone we know," Dennis whispered, the color rising from his throat to his face, his hand slowly closing into tender fists. "What—What are we going to do about it?" He pushed back his chair, ready.

"No," Valjean said, drawing a firm line, then smudging it a little with a laugh and a headshake. "Not you." She gathered their plates and carried them into the kitchen. She could hear Carpenter telling Dennis, "Someone saw Gannett's boys on the logging road yesterday afternoon. I'll step on down that way and see what they know."

"But Carpenter—" She returned with sudsy hands to prevent.

He pulled Valjean to him, muting all outcry with his brandied breath. He pleased himself with a kiss, taking his time, winking a galvanized-gray eye at Dennis. "I'm just going to talk to them. About time they knew me better."

She looked so miserable standing there that he caught her to him again, boyish, lean; the years had rolled off of him, leaving him uncreased, and no scars that showed. He had always been lucky, folks said. Wild lucky.

"Listen here now," he warned. "Trust me?"

What answer would serve but yes? She spoke it after

a moment, for his sake, with all her heart, like a charm to cast out fear. "Of course."

Dennis, wheeling his bike out to head down to Mrs. Cobb's for his music lesson, knelt to make some minor adjustment on the chain.

"I won't be long," Carpenter said. "Take care of yourselves."

"You too," Dennis called, and pedaled off.

Carpenter crouched and pulled on his stiff, cleaned boots, then hefted one foot gaily into a shaft of sunset, admiring the shine. "Good work, ma'am." He tipped an imaginary hat and strode off into the shadows of the tall pines.

A whippoorwill startled awake and shouted once, then sleepily subsided. Overhead the little brown bats tottered and strove through the first starlight, their high twittering falling like tiny blown kisses onto the wind-scoured woods. It was very peaceful there in the deep heart of the April evening, and it had to be a vagrant, unworthy, warning impulse that sent Valjean prowling to the cabinet in the den where they kept their tax records, warranties, brandy, and side arms. Trembling, she reached again and again, but couldn't find the pistol. Carpenter's pistol wasn't there.

Not there.

For a moment she would not believe it, just rested her head against the cool shelf; then she turned and ran, leaving lights on and doors open behind her, tables and rugs askew in her wake. She ran sock-footed toward trouble as straight as she could, praying *Carpenter! Carpenter!* with every step. And then, like answered prayer, he was there, sudden as something conjured up from the dark. He caught her by the shoulders and shook her into sense.

"What's happened? Babe? What is it?"

But she could not answer for laughing and crying both at once, to see him there safe, to meet him half-way. When she caught her breath she said, "I was afraid something awful— I thought— I didn't know if I'd ever—"

"I told you I was just going to talk with them," he chided, amused. She gave a skip to get in step beside him. He caught her hand up and pointed her own finger at her. "I thought you said you trusted me."

"But I didn't know you were taking the gun with you . . ."

Angry, he drew away. She felt the night chill raise the hair on the back of her neck.

"I didn't take the damn gun! What makes you say things like that? You think I'm some kind of nut?"

"But it's gone," she protested. "I looked."

And then a new specter rose between them, unspeakable, contagious. For a moment they neither moved nor spoke, then Carpenter started for home, fast, outdistancing her in a few strides. Over his shoulder he called back, edgy, unconvinced, "You missed it, that's all. It's there." He would make sure.

She ran but could not quite catch up. "Dennis has it," she accused Carpenter's back.

"Nah," he shouted. "Don't borrow trouble. It's home."

When he loped across the lawn and up the kitchen steps three at a time he was a full minute ahead of her. And when she got there Carpenter was standing in the doorway of the den empty-handed, with the rapt, calculating, baffled expression of a baby left holding a suddenly limp string when the balloon has burst and vanished. The phone was ringing, ringing.

"Answer it," he said into the dark, avoiding her eyes.

Hindsight

They met after a rock concert. She had lost sight of the friends she had come with, and her rabbity glance, seeking a landmark face in the multitude, encountered his, a stranger's, then moved on, still seeking. Then found him again. He stood alone on the periphery of the flowing crowd that propelled her toward him. He reached for her, pulled her toward him by the small silver cross at her throat, drew her close enough to be heard. She shook her head and giggled, "I'll miss my ride."

"D'you ever go ninety miles per, with nothing between you and your fears but black wind?"

She laughed as though she understood.

It was her first motorcycle ride. To hear her squeal, he shut off the headlamp and drove blind on the causeway. He laid the machine almost over on its pegs as he rounded the last corner and drove across the lawn and up the walk to deliver her into the circle of her mother's porch light. He didn't stay. She could hear him ripping back down G Street; he must have made all the lights; he didn't stop. She trembled up the stairs to bed, still smiling. He had her phone number written on the thigh of his jeans. During study hall she wrote *I love Steve, I love Steve, I love Steve* on the soles of her tennis shoes. A summer's beachcombing erased it heel and toe, and his motorcycle pegs wore it off under the arches. By Labor Day they were engaged.

When they had satisfied the Church that they were prepared for the sacrament of holy matrimony, they married. She was eighteen. After not quite a year she gave birth to a daughter who coughed, gurgled a moment only, then died. The priest infiltrated her twilight sleep to break the news and to tell her that it was all right, God did not mind, she had not entirely failed for she had fulfilled her obligation to try, and no doubt would have another chance soon. Her husband, nervous, silent, chain-smoking at the waiting-room window, watched cars as they went by, going elsewhere. Thereafter, occasionally, with increasing frequency, he too was elsewhere.

The child was never mentioned. It had its fate, no reality. She never got to hold it. No one could understand her lingering depression, which was her only remaining defense, for it seemed to her that every vulnerability in herself had been found out, examined in the merciless committee work of priestly counsel. To all complaints and sighs came the exhortation: try again, try harder. She confessed her suspicions about her husband: her sisters and their husbands, with their sharp eyes and vantages and biases, reported his drinking, his late evenings spent in the company of rowdy bikers and potheads. This too, the priest said, was her fault. She had driven him away with her coldness; she should examine herself and determine how, then try harder.

She was to win him back; she was to want him back. But he didn't see it that way. When she most sincerely and valiantly tried, he abused her. Once he knocked her down. She asked the priest to forgive her for provoking him, for she had learned, had finally learned, the rules of the game. And of course she tried again.

Despite all chances for disillusion she remained an innocent, a dreamwalker. When would she wake? Her best friend from school asked her to stand with her when she married and confided later how her husband's clan demanded the "cloth of proof" after the wedding night. She did not understand; she went to her sisters and asked, her sisters with their crammed houses stinking of boiled dinners and damp wash and poxy children. They teased her into retreat. She walked home in the rain, blushes (How could I be so stupid?) steaming on her cheeks. All her life it had been like that; being the youngest by half a dozen years, everyone got the joke before she did, understood everything before she did, years ahead, so she must hasten to catch up, or fake it, laughing along in ignorance. They knew it all before she did, from long division to menarche. Their competency awed her, silenced her, and her silence had been her shield against ridicule . . . All the way home she was saying, "Why am I such a fool?" and when she got home, her husband was entertaining someone in their bed. She turned and fled into the rain again, finally taking refuge in the Church. Incoherent, she humbly confessed her total failure as a wife and prayed for death. At nineteen.

The priest and his seniors, rung by diocesan rung to the highest, consulted. The marriage (so the decision filtered down) was not to be set aside; it was a sacrament and had left its certain indelible mark on their souls.

They went for counseling. Her husband, in an ugly scene, boasted that he had married to avoid the draft and the child had been meant to make that avoidance absolute. But the war ended, and with it, all necessity.

He didn't need her; he'd be glad to be rid of her . . .
She fainted (shock and anemia). The priest looked a
little pale himself. The Church tried again. Up and up
went the petition.

Meanwhile she went to live with her mother, holing
up in the attic room from whose diamond pane she
had watched as a child to see her father, roaring
drunk, back the truck down the alley with its latest load
of illogical firewood—perhaps a canted chicken coop,
perhaps a piano. All to be axed into submission while
he caroled at the top of his Irish lungs. Dead now,
from complications. So the empty house had plenty of
room, but she retreated to the attic, lying on her
maiden bed, listening to the season pass. She slept
hours at a time, days at a time, weeks. Her mother
brought her meals (mostly uneaten), gossip from the
street (it rolled off the wax of her alienation like rain),
a priest (she excommunicated him), nieces (she held
them on her gaunt lap and wept into their hair),
Christmas cards (not many), birthday cards (she turned
twenty), and finally a phone number (a lawyer's).

She had no savings. Her husband had cleaned it all
out and wasn't to be found. She sold her rings for what
she could get (not enough) and her sisters and her
mother took up a collection among themselves, shaving
grocery money and tithes, keeping their own counsel,
going without, so that she could go . . . to El Paso on
the day coach, all arranged, one fee covered all, everything arranged. She was met at the airport by the *abogado* and his wife. They made all the explanations as
they crossed the bridge into Juárez over the shining
river. The customs officials made only a cursory exami-
nation. She had never been even one hundred miles
from home, and now this, another country, accompa-
nied by strangers whose purchased kindness might fail

at any time. They drove to the hotel where her residency requirements would be accomplished; they drove away and left her, saying they would pick her up in the morning for some sightseeing, and paperwork, at their offices in a nearby street. That would be fine? Yes, yes, she nodded, pretending poise: her life's work.

The hotel clerk jangled the keys and she followed him to her room. He called her *señorita* and said, "Any little thing?" and when he left she locked the door behind him. She felt the whole building tremble (she feared at first it was an earthquake) as the elevator whirred and plunged back down to earth, and she made up her mind that she would take the stairs when she went back down for supper, included in the blanket fee.

Her eyes watered and stung from the glare of the ride into Mexico, from the shimmer of the whitewashed buildings and tin roofs. She set her overnight case on the stained, cigarette-scarred dresser and avoided her reflection in the wavery mirror. She yawned. She threw back the lank coverlet and lay, clothed and shod, on the jaded mattress. Down in the street in the day's heat, life raged on, like the song of cicadas. She was tired but not sleepy. The noise and heat oppressed her. With the window open, she felt vulnerable. With it shut, she suffocated. Her head ached. She had not brought aspirin.

It had sounded so easy when they explained it: fly down, cross the border, spend the night, cross back home, fly north again, freed. Free.

She picked up the phone.

¿Sí, señorita? (Insolent perhaps? Knowing? Sly?)

"Aspirin. Do you have anything for headache? Aspirin tablets?" She spoke in broken syllables to make herself understood. Was she understood? Would he bring her aspirin?

¡Sí señorita!

But an hour passed and nothing happened. She un-locked the door and went down, by the stairs, avoiding the cranky, dark elevator. The clerk looked up. She did not know if he was the same one who checked her in. Was he the one who took her call?

"Aspirin," she enunciated.

Ah, sí, sí, duele la cabeza, sí, he agreed. Was he going to help her? Uncomprehending, she advanced across the lobby with its palms, once venerable, now in a sea-son of molt and despair. A man slept behind his news-paper at the window with its trapped flies. The fake leather of the chairs caught the afternoon's light in old impressions of anonymous waiting flesh. The fan, overhead, was still. People, place, furnishings had come down in the world so gradually that they still had their pride.

The clerk, when she came to the desk, put out his hand and insinuated, *Señorita is lonely?* in English good enough. She fled back upstairs, ran the chain in its channel, and turned the lock. She had left the window open and her purse in plain sight. She hurried to it and checked—everything was there. Relieved, she se-cured the window. As she stood there a man in the street, looking up, caught her eye and made a gesture in whatever language comprehensible. She drew the shade.

She had a growing horror of everything in the room, of its probable past, its likely uncleanliness, its unrigh-teousness. This was her Purgatory; she had cast herself into it; she must bide here a while. She splashed water from the reluctant tap onto her hands, her face, care-ful not to let any drop of it pass her lips.

The phone rang. Was it the lawyer and his wife? She answered on an outrush of grateful breath, "Yes?"

The clerk? Someone else? A man. The one sleeping in the lobby? The one in the street? A stranger, accented: "May I come up?" She hung up.

Later, within the hour, another call. The lawyer's wife. "You all well and happy? All okay?"

What could she say? "All okay," she hoped.

"Tomorrow we pick up, ready on the time early?"

"Yes oh yes."

Night came, the same stars shining there that shine down on all the flags of the world, but the sky looked alien to her. In the street, past midnight, the same loud living: talk, arguments, parting, arrivals, jokes, despairs, threats, and barking of dogs, as though the town ran on a twenty-four hour clock. In the corridors beyond her bolted door, perpetual footsteps, whisperings, bargainings. She lay unblinking on the bed and wondered if she should pray. For what? For her immortal soul with its certain indelible marks? For her daughter who breathed only twice? For her failures? For her success? The Church had left her; she had left the Church. Suppose within two years they granted her an official annulment; by then it would be worth what to her? Who would she be? It wasn't anger she felt; it was a quietness, as though there had been a final argument and things had been said that couldn't be unsaid, things that outweighed love. The priest had said . . .

The phone waked her from confusion, not sleep. From her terror of waiting. "Yes?"

A long silence, then a man's rough offer. In Spanish? In German? In Latin? She did not know. She flung down the phone and paced, then moved the dresser, inched it over the cracked linoleum to bar the door, to fortify her position. She trembled from the effort, from the necessity, from hunger. She had not dared go down to the lobby and into the restaurant to eat. She

chewed her last stick of gum and checked the time.
Her watch was gone! Fallen as she moved the dresser.
She crawled on hands and knees, patting into shadows,
listening to its tick, finding it. It had suffered. Its
hands stood still. It began to lie. She buckled it on
anyway and from hour to hour sought its opinion,
however incredible, out of old habit. She lay down
again, waiting. Songs and laughter from the street below. Traffic and heat unabated. The monotonous
barking of dogs. Church bells.

Morning came. She stood ready. At the *señora's*
knock and voice, she moved the dresser back in place
and unlocked. They went downstairs, out past the clerk
(same one? new one?) and into the morning with its
scant freshness on the stale dust, nothing so virginal as
dew . . . Perhaps spit, perhaps tears.

They rode in the car to the *abogado's* where, in the
small glassed cubicle, she signed papers. She had already signed papers. She would sign more papers. She
listened again to the explanations and then handed
over the check, her eyes resting themselves in that distant place on her mother's countersignature. After the
business was accomplished, they rode around, just
around, killing time.

No, she wasn't hungry. (Everywhere the rancid smell
of cooking oil.)

Here and there, over a crumbling wall, flowers on
strange, unkind stems, daring her to near with swords
drawn. Traffic paused to honor the slow pedestrian
file of patient mourners trailing an infant's shouldered
coffin. She lay back, eyes closed, till the procession
passed and they drove on. They put in the necessary
hours. She drank a Coke. She was resident that legaliz-
ing while, then on the exact hour they headed for the
bridge, her papers in order. They opened her little

green overnight case with its cargo of pink nylon to the sky, like a melon. The officer snapped it shut with a smile and a salute. Welcome home. There on the far bank, the American flag. Seeing it, she burst into tears. The same flag that stood in the corner of the dark stage between assemblies all through high school. The same flag that sagged on its rusty pole over the post office in her hometown. She noticed it for the first time. She said she would remember.

Back home she handed the papers to the American lawyer, and eventually they went through. She was free. The Church, after a time, granted the annulment. Her Bulova, when it returned from the shop, was again in step. There was only that little scratch on its face, indelible, a scar. Resetting it, she made new appointments. She saw her husband (now legally and in the eyes of the Church a stranger) on the shore road, on his motorcycle, going fast. Going, it turned out, away. She only recognized him in the rearview mirror, after he had passed. When it was too late.

Inexorable Progress

There's not much difference between a bare tree and a dead tree in winter. Only when the others begin to leaf out the next spring and one is left behind in the general green onrush can the eye tell. By then it is too late for remedy. That's how it was with Angelina: a tree stripped to the natural bone, soul-naked in the emptying wind. She was good at pretending; she hung color and approximations of seasonal splendor on every limb, and swayed like a bower in the autumn gales around her, but her heart was hollow, and her nests empty. You could tell a little something by her eyes, with their devious candor (like a drunk's), but her troubles, whatever they were, didn't start with the bottle, and after a while the bottle wasn't what stopped them.

Glory be to the Father she sang the Sunday before Labor Day. She wore her neckline low, her hem and heels and spirits as high as fashion and propriety would allow.

and to the Son and to the Holy Ghost
When she warbled in the sanctuary, her freckled bosom rippled in vibrato. She left no fingerprints on the salver as she dropped in her tithe.

as it was in the beginning

She kept herself retouched, forever presenting the same bright portrait to the saints.

is now and ever shall be

Her cordial eyes, fixed in bravado, were shining windows, bolted against bad weather.

world without end, amen

Behind them, fear, that restless housecat, paced.

amen.

She hated many things, but Sundays most of all.

The congregation settled in for the sermon now that it was paid for. To her daughter beside her Angelina whispered, "Listen, Bon"—as though she were still a fidgety child, impervious as stone, around whose innocence the words and water of life would pour unproved; as though Bonnie were still six, to be cajoled into rectitude (or at least silence) with carefully doled bribes of Lifesavers tasting of the scented depths of her purse.

Part of what Angelina hated about Sundays was sitting alone in church while her husband went fishing or hunting. The way he saw it, he always made it up to her afterward, but from black-powder season to doe days she might as well have been a widow. Of course, Bonnie was growing up there beside her, but it wasn't the same. To make sure nobody thought she was getting resigned to it, or ever would, Angelina always reserved a space beside her in the pew, so the world would know at a glance that Chick was expected back.

Sometimes she thought more than was reasonable about who was missing. Sometimes she dreamed about her stillborn son; every month just before her period she dreamed about him. Perhaps he was just born and they laid him wailing, wriggling, on her belly. Or perhaps he was a little older, running to her with a pine-cone pipe, calling, "See what I found? Come see!" She always recognized him, who he would have been. Once she dreamed they were camping in hunting season and he came fretting up, arms out in a "Love me, love me, mama" pose, and she gave him a bloody fox foot to teethe on, to hush him. She never told Chick about the dreams, nor what it was she had been suffering in her sleep when she cried, "Help!" and woke them both.

Here lately she had been dreaming about her mother; always the same thing: just before they sealed the coffin (her mother had died in April) she saw her mama's eyelids flicker; no one believed her (suddenly everybody was a stranger; dark-suited, efficient, looming, they closed ranks against her, and she cried "Stop!" but they did not stop), and the inexorable progress toward the dark, the sealing, the lowering, the losing sight of, the closing went on until she woke herself dry-mouthed, heart-pounding, telling herself it was only a dream. Its persistence shamed her, haunted her; she could not tell anyone how she felt, that she had got off too light, that she deserved worse than heartbreak. She had felt that way from the beginning; indeed, had tried to comfort the comforters at the funeral. The feeling of guilt, of some punishment deserved, haunted her through the summer until one night she dreamed she had a pain in her left breast, and the sensation of pain woke her like a noise, like a light. She lay panting in fright, unable to disbelieve, or perhaps unwilling. Waking fully, she investigated and found a lump: a dream come true. It somehow satisfied her; it was her secret. She would not see a doctor; she knew how it went. Her mother had died of such a lump. Sometimes Angelina imagined herself wasted like that; when she raised her own hand before her eyes she saw her mother's skeleton instead.

Angelina lost her appetite. She began cleaning out

closets. During a rainy spell she got out the carton of snapshots and began putting them in an album for Bonnie, labeling who and what and when. She smoked heavily (Bonnie always after her to quit, saying, "Mama, I want you around") and the fruitcake brandy (a bottle had lasted five years) vanished in one afternoon. When Elsie Bland and her boy Jude came in the afternoon to pick windfall apples on shares, Angelina crouched close against the kitchen cabinet, out of sight, while they knocked and knocked. After a while they went away. When Bonnie got home from school, she found her mama rubber-legged, penitent, incapacitated. Bonnie cleaned her up, mopped, ran the laundry through, and had the place aired out and sweet-smelling when Chick got home. They called it the flu that time; there were other times . . .

Lost in reverie, Angelina did not realize the service was over; Bonnie was touching her arm and saying, "Mama? Mama!" and it made her start. She stood perhaps too quickly, for she had to stop a moment, resting her hand on the rubbed pew-end till the stained glass on her periphery swung and settled. Then she walked down (it seemed uphill) the burgundy carpet in which her sharp heels picked little dimples, and out into the dazzling sunlight, her left hand holding up the bulletin to fend off the noon. Reverend Martin made his small remarks at the door, gentle pleasantries served with a handshake to each departing member. He was speaking to Angelina, but she couldn't make out the words. All around her thrummed an expectant, dimming silence like the instant between lightning and thunder. She turned away, troubled, from the lips soundlessly moving, and shut her eyes against the intolerable glare off the whited church front. Very suddenly the porch tilted up and she

pitched down the steps, unconscious before she relin-
quished the Reverend's hand, which is why (the doctor said later) there were no bones broken.

She told the doctor some of what she had been going
through: not the dreams, not the brandy. He gave her
something for her nerves and arranged for a biopsy on
the lump. Overnight in the hospital, and she would
know for sure (but she *was* sure!). Chick gave up a
bow-and-arrow weekend to be with her; he was what
she saw when she opened her eyes after the surgery;
he was the one who exulted, "Benign." But she didn't
believe him. Hadn't they lied to her mother? Finally,
finally they persuaded her.

Relieved, yet oddly disappointed, she went home determined to make the most of her spared life. At Sun-
day-night services she laid her cigarettes on the altar
rail and asked for prayer to help her kick the habit.
Dust gathered on the unopened conscience bottle of
brandy. She built up to four miles of brisk walking
every morning and was able to sleep without medication. She took up crafts, and began hooking a rug for
Bonnie's room. ("Do something for yourself," Bonnie
said, when her mama finished that and began a matching pillow, but Angelina said, "Doing for others, that's
the reason we're here.")

The doctors advised her to cut out caffeine too and
she was able to break a fourteen-cup-a-day habit. ("Jesus can fix anything," she told her neighbor as they
jogged in the fine fall weather.) For her forty-third
birthday Chick bought her a hair-fine chain with a gold
charm: PERFEC$_T$ it announced. She fastened it on and
wore it along with the little silver cross her mother left
her. She was on a streak of pure happiness.

But, of course, there is no such thing unalloyed.
Cakes fall. Cars break down. A roofing staple manages

to penetrate the week-old radial. The eggs on the top shelf of the refrigerator freeze. Dogs, even the most kindly treated, chase cats, wander, bark well off cue. Bills get lost in the mails. Angelina's streak ended with vapor lock. She had been shopping for groceries for the week; they and milk and frozen foods were in the trunk when the car cut out. She had an appointment in an hour, so she took a shortcut in repairs; rather than wait for the car to cool, she ran in the bait shop and bought a bag of ice and held it to the hot engine, and the engine block cracked. Still, she expected sympathy, not a scolding, and could hardly believe it when Chick roared up behind the wrecker and jumped out and began yelling, "How can you be so goddam stupid!" before God and the gathering crowd. And while he was on the subject, why didn't she wash her car once in a while? A little soap in a bucket of water wouldn't kill her . . .

She pointed out (while the wrecker hooked up) that she might have more motivation if the car were in her name. (Nothing was—not the house, not the lot at Hammermill, nor the pontoon, nothing. "I bet if I polished the Revereware I'd find his Social Security number engraved on the bottom," she fumed later.) She rode in the wrecker, wouldn't ride with Chick.

"A thousand bucks for a new engine," he told her as she climbed into the wrecker. "You want it fixed, *you* earn it." As though what she did, what she was, wasn't worth anything to him! To say it like that before the wide world! If he meant it, about her paying for the repairs, he only meant it when he said it, not a moment later, but it pleased Angelina to prolong the quarrel. Nothing he thought to do could stop it now. It must run its course, like a disease.

Tuesday was election day. Angelina had been on her

way to the courthouse to be sworn in as poll chief for Deerfield when the car tore up and she and Chick boiled over. Grace Arnold had had to be the one to run up to Hammermill for the materials. She offered Angelina a ride election day, too, and came by before six-thirty that morning with her car loaded with supplies (extension cord, flag, posterboard, hampers of lunch and magazines, folding chairs). Angelina was waiting at the foot of the drive with a look of righteous malice on her face; she got in bragging what she had done (looking a little scared too): she had locked Chick's truck in the garage, along with the ladder, and had thrown both sets of keys up on the roof, as high as indignation would allow.

How he solved the problem Grace never knew, but he came in to vote around noon. They had the precinct set up in the Fish and Game Clubhouse, the old schoolhouse on the pine hill, high enough so you could see the traffic passing by on the road; the magnolia blocked the north view, but you could see the cars a half-mile off looking south, and Grace, with her bright eye, spotted the blue truck and said, "Isn't that Chick?" Instantly, Angelina fled. They could hear her in back, dropping incorrect change through the Coke machine, over and over. Grace signed Chick up and he voted; it didn't take very long. When the curtains swept open and he emerged, cheerful with done duty, he glanced all around, encountering nowhere his wife. He didn't inquire.

"All right then," he said, pocketing his hands and staring out the window toward the reservoir where a yellow boat sped along. It looked like Chick might be going to announce something, but he didn't, just mentioned the weather, and went on out jingling his keys loudly enough so that if you were listening and interested in the back of the building, you could hear them. He cast another proud look at the sky as he got into his truck, as though it were all his doing, as though he had invented blue.

"He said, 'Have a nice day,' " Grace told Angelina when she came back to her chair.

"A *good* day," Angelina corrected. "He didn't mean me." She gave a little laugh, a single bark of desperation.

At the end of the day they closed the door, took down the notices of penalties and warnings, counted and recapped, signed the quadruplicate forms, sorted the papers into the proper envelopes, posted the results, and loaded the stuff (chairs, cushions, crochet, magazines, thermoses, flag, and extension cord) into Grace's car and headed for the courthouse at Hammermill. The key to the Fish and Game Clubhouse stayed between times in the cash register at Bully's store, so they stopped by there and Angelina ran in with it. When she came back out, she had a shock: it felt like terror; it felt like triumph. There was Chick, his truck parked alongside Grace's car on the far side of the gas pumps. Without a pause or hitch Angelina got back into Grace's Monte Carlo as though she hadn't *seen*, but Grace knew better.

"Aw, honey, can't you budge just a little?" Grace cried. "Please! I'll take care of this." She patted the official boxes with the state seals on the side. Angelina hesitated. Almost too long.

They heard Chick's truck crank, final offer.

At the last possible instant Angelina jumped out and ran across, leaning a little forward on her wedgies as though battling head winds. Chick offered her a hand up, but she ignored it. When they drove out, Angelina was stiff-backed, eyes shut. Chick hung a vehement right onto the road home, tipping her over against his

shoulder. "Thanky ma'am," he said. He had that ener-
gized look he always wore when he had a secret; Angelina suspected some grand gesture; perhaps he had
bought her another car . . .

But when they got home (and they rode, after his
'thanky,' without speaking, in an uneasy truce) it wasn't
a new car at all. They had cooked supper and done the
laundry, that was the surprise. They had helped out.
Bonnie stood with the sheets in her arms and Chick
went over to help her fold them. Were they waiting for
praise? Angelina looked at the table with its little bouquet of persimmon leaves and oak and sourwood.
Candles, too, and Sunday dishes. Everything in its proper place. They didn't need her, that's what they were
saying! They could get along without her! (She mentioned that.)

Bonnie's stricken face in the candlelight was more
than Angelina could bear.

"Don't 'Mama, please,' me! I've had enough of your
whining about how things ought to be! It's not going to
be 'Mommy and Daddy' on their wedding cake, and
Santa, and the Easter Bunny like a roof over you, and
happily ever after all your life! The roof leaks. It blows
off in chunks. It rots. It stinks! You have to save yourself, don't you 'Mama, Mama' me, don't you 'Now Angelina, honey,' me!" She jerked her shoulder from
Chick's grasp and sent herself to bed without supper.
To punish herself or them? She lay wondering as the
codeine in her migraine medication took effect.

Later she woke in terror and loneliness. The house
was so silent all around her. She put out her hand and
Chick was there; he hadn't left her; he hadn't given up
on her. He wanted her. A real treaty, mouth to mouth,
was signed. In the morning she made a last-minute call
to the Avon lady (order was going in that day) for that

chain and charm necklace Bonnie had admired, a peace offering. And she gave in about music camp. She told Bonnie that afternoon, said they'd just have to learn to get along without Bonnie this once, even if it was Thanksgiving, since it meant so much to the girl. She helped her fill out the forms (a church-run retreat): *Who is the most influential person in your life?* Bonnie paused at that blank and considered. Angelina had absolutely no doubt.

"Jesus Christ," she told her. "Write it in."

Bonnie, who had been about to write *parents*, blushed, ashamed she had not even thought of it.

"Write it in," Angelina said again. Bonnie wrote.

After Christmas Angelina canvassed door to door, handing out pamphlets ("ERA—The Trojan Horse"), saying till she was numb, "I'm Mrs. Chester Cole, I'd like to speak with you a few moments on a subject vital to the survival of the American home and leave you some literature to study." Mixed results.

"You Jehovah's Witness?" The woman peered out through the rusty screen, reaching for the pamphlet, holding it to the sun, studying the illustrated cover. "Are you for or against?"

And Angelina said, "I hope you'll read and then pass it on to your friends; write your congressmen and legislators—"

"Them Jehovah's Witness stay and stay. I tell her, 'Lady, please, my carrots is scorching,' but she just sits like she never smelled smoke."

"If you or your friends have any questions—"

"Mormon fellers the same. Nice-looking boys prayed and prayed on me. Left me a whole book to read. Say they coming back."

"I thank you for your time," Angelina said.

At another house she tried to interest the woman in joining the bus rally to the capitol.

"Shoot, I got me a job, ma'am. You let someone else have my seat." She handed the pamphlet back. "I'm only home today because of the flu. Head's aching so bad I can't read."

"And thank you for your time," Angelina said.

When she stopped by Grace's for more brochures, Grace reminded her about printing costs.

"So you think I'm throwing them out of an airplane over the reservoir?" Angelina pried off her boots and rested her legs on the coffee table. "Although I might as well . . ." She rubbed her ankles. "Just look. Mama's feet did the same, swelled so they nearly burst. Be so much easier to *phone*."

Grace kept on counting out pamphlets. She had something new, a Xeroxed page from the *Congressional Record*. "A copy for each field worker," she said, handing Angelina hers.

"You ever get the idea what's the use?" Angelina wondered.

"Tomorrow we're going to run off another thousand 'Things You Can Do' fact sheets . . ."

"Nobody listens," Angelina said. "You ever notice?"

"—getting some of those bumper stickers and litter bags (did I show you those? around here somewhere) and maybe get some of those—"

"I guess you never did notice," Angelina decided. "I bet I could tell you I was going home and pipe a bottle of Valium and sleep till the daisies sprung and you'd say—"

"—like stop signs, real cute; they're red and say STOP; we could pass them out at the bank on Saturday."

Angelina zipped her boots back on and stood up. "May I quote you? And you'd say . . ."

"Why anything you can use," Grace said, flattered,

smiling, puzzling it out. (Something like that, if you remember it later, is the only hint you get, the kind of joke the whole world makes one down day or another.)

But Angelina didn't have her mind made up; she was still trying. She made lists of things to get done, lists for the day, the week, the month; goals for the coming year. She drove over to the house and went through her mother's clothes, one closet at a time, and made all these decisions without crying for help, or receiving any. She had the trunk and the backseat of her Maverick (Chick got the engine rebuilt before Christmas) crammed with sacks and boxes for Goodwill and was on her way there, Ash Wednesday, when she had more car trouble. This wasn't like the old trouble; this time the car stalled and she couldn't get it to re-start. She coasted down to the stop sign at the corner and set the brake, resting her head on the wheel and considering her luck. She rolled her window down and wished she had a cigarette. It was unsettling to be sitting there stalled, with the faint scent of her mother's household all around her. Was it a sign she wasn't supposed to get rid of all the stuff? She decided to walk home. It wasn't half a mile.

As she got out, a voice said, "I thought it was you. I've been watching you. What were you doing, praying?"

Angelina whirled around and there stood Ginnie Daniels, in pristine Adidas, with a dry sweatband holding back her hair. She pressed her hand on the stitch in her side.

"That Roy. I told him I couldn't keep up. Maybe I lied when I said I was doing three miles a day, but he promised to go slow, then he said never mind. Said he'd go on without me. And he did!"

"I'd offer you a lift," Angelina said, "but my car's conked out."

"Maybe it's flooded," Ginnie said. "Maybe you flooded it." She walked over and reached in and gave the hood latch a yank. "Let's see."

They stood there listening to the oil drip back into the pan.

"You know something about cars?" Angelina hoped.

"Me?" Ginnie blew a pink bubble. "Nah." She spelled F-O-X-Y in the dust on the air cleaner, careful of her nails. She noticed the gold charm at Angelina's throat and pointed at it. "Going to get me one of those. Maybe the one that says *10*."

Reminded, Angelina raised her hand to her throat and touched the little cross. "Do you believe in prayer?" she asked, with that incandescent look people had about gotten used to.

Ginnie blinked and formed another bubble, enlarging it slowly to cosmic proportions. It burst. "Couldn't hurt."

Angelina laid her hands on certain blue objects under the hood. Then she got in and turned the key. The car cranked instantly.

Ginnie slammed the hood. "Praise the Lord anyway," she drawled, settling herself on the seat, propping her feet on the dash. "You can drop me off at the light in town."

"I can remember when you were born," Angelina said as Ginnie lit a cigarette. "I went to your mama's shower."

"Yeah?"

"It goes so fast."

"The faster the better . . . I'm getting me a T-roof Z for graduation," Ginnie said. She made a gesture of running through gears. "We're already planning what to do. Not going to spray SENIORS on the bridges or LEGALIZE POT on the water tower . . . Kid stuff . . . They'll remember us a while . . . Raise us a little hell . . . Going down to Daytona, Lauderdale maybe . . ."

Angelina frowned, remembering. "Our class went to Panama City."

"Bet you had a ball," Ginnie said indulgently.

"One of the boys hit a cow in the rain. Wiped out his brand-new T-bird. The girl with him went right through the windshield. It blinded her. Broke Danny's neck, they said instantly."

"Yeah?" Ginnie shook her head. "Wow." She pointed up ahead. "This is my corner." When they stopped, Ginnie got out and stretched. "Beats jogging. Thanks a bunch for the lift." She hipped the door shut.

"Something always happens," Angelina realized.

"Ma'am?" Ginnie peered back in at her.

"Death," Angelina said.

When she got home from the trip to Goodwill, JoJo was missing. The dog didn't come in for supper, and in the night when Angelina got up and walked around the yard, calling, there was no sign of him. He had never stayed out all night before.

"If only I had locked him the garage when I left!" Angelina, pacing, making coffee, calling, and the lights on managed to rouse the household. Bonnie stood in the glare of the kitchen and pled for her mama not to get upset.

"Why do you think it's you? Why do you have to be the one?" Bonnie asked.

"Because I'm guilty," Angelina said simply. "Who else is to blame?"

Chick stood in the door, backlit, haloed by moths, and called to Angelina out wandering in the yard to come to bed, to be sensible. But she had to take the lantern and search along the roadside for his body, if he had been hit by a car . . . She didn't find him.

From the first they ruled out stealth; he wasn't the

sort of dog you'd kidnap for ransom. He was a stray mutt puppy who required so much medical attention when he took up with them that it kept Angelina's mind off the stillbirth of their son. She sometimes bragged that JoJo's vet bills ran as much as a pediatrician's, and early on, when Chick, holding up the silly little green sweater she had crocheted for the dog, teased, "Without JoJo, Bonnie would be an only child," Angelina's sudden tears washed the remarks completely away. Now she couldn't shake the feeling that her prayer to get the Maverick going (but hadn't she said *Thy* will?) had cost her the dog.

"Christ's sake, it's nobody's fault!" Chick said. He pretended not to worry, but she heard him in the woods whistling the come-here-boy note that JoJo had always run to. They searched for a week, night and day, patrolling the near roads and calling, calling. When Chick said, "Face it," and Bonnie said, "He was getting old," Angelina said, "Was? Was!" and went on looking, after Bonnie went to school, after Chick drove away to work. She walked early. Later, she and her jogging partner made the rounds; no clues, no telltale ravens, nothing.

The Friday before Palm Sunday was frosty. Angelina was jogging alone and she smelled something. She tried to kid herself, but she cut the run short and with growing dread followed the old wagon road to the hilltop. There was a springhouse, fallen in for years, smothered in vinca and lilies in season. The pool was dark and leaf-clotted. That's where he lay; that's where JoJo had died. It might have been his heart; it might have been poison. What difference now?

He lay with his head a little way over the lip of the pool. After considering, she decided to take only his collar; his collar and tags only would she salvage for burial. When she touched him, it surprised her; he was warm. A little steam rose from his body, the work of worms. She caught the leather of the collar in her hands and began to unfasten it. The unforeseen: as she tried to slip the collar off, the dog's head detached itself and fell ripely into her hands. Angelina caught it. She tried to put it back. Tried beyond reason to put it back. She cried out and stood and stomped and shook herself free of the maggots which had climbed past her elbows. She scooped the collar out of the water and ran, ran without looking back.

Chick took care of it that night. When he asked if she wanted the collar buried in the little grove of dog-woods, Angelina didn't care.

Sometime during the week of Easter, Angelina made up her mind. On Wednesday after Easter she took Chick's good dark suit to the cleaners and on the way home she stopped in the Van Shop to buy a replace-ment windbreaker for Bonnie, who had left hers on the school bus again—the third one the girl had lost. Chick had said, "Let her do without," the only way to teach her. "But here I am again," Angelina told the clerk.

"Same with my kids," the clerk agreed. "What would they do without us?"

Angelina considered that a moment, her pen poised above the check. "I don't know," she admitted. She signed her name gravely, as to a warrant, as though lives and honor were at stake. The sound the check made as she tore it from the book, that papery final complaint made her sad. Tears stung her eyes.

"Going to be pretty today. Even prettier tomorrow. Not a cloud in the— Oops, spoke too soon," the clerk said, pointing. Shoulder to shoulder they examined the sky through the amber sun film.

"That cloud's looking for me," Angelina laughed. "I washed my car." She laughed, as though she recognized it of old. The heavy door with its COME ON IN decal and cowbell swung shut behind her. The clerk called, "See you," and Angelina raised her hand.

She drove home and got there in time to answer the phone: Grace reminding her about the Tupperware party. "Two-thirty," Grace said. "A little early so we can talk. Been missing you lately."

"Two-thirty," Angelina lied.

She wrote a note and with the TODAY IS THE FIRST DAY magnet pinned it to Thursday: *Blue suit ready at noon.* She wrote it in red to catch Chick's eye. He would be needing that suit.

She wasn't hungry, hadn't eaten all day. She felt light-headed and breezy, the way she had felt when she was about to be married, when she knew the tremendous doom and peace of being sure, of knowing her fate, of being espoused, and trusting her choice. She sat in Chick's chair, with its shape martyred to his. She could faintly smell his hairdressing. She reached toward the little table and turned on the reading lamp. The Bible fell open to the place she had marked with a rose from her mother's funeral blanket. She read, then in the center of a clean page of paper she made a note, folded it, sealed it in an envelope. She wasn't going to mail it; she didn't need a stamp. She left it on the table.

After that, she filled the bird feeder which the squirrels had raided again. She walked down to the mailbox and read the weekly news on her way back up the drive. There was a pine cone on the steps; she picked it up and dropped it in the kindling bin. There were handprints on the refrigerator; she buffed them away and put up the rag. It was time to be on her way.

Angelina glanced around the house; everything was tidy. She picked up her pocketbook and went out. In a moment she unlocked and went back in, to check if she had unplugged the coffee maker (she had), and after that she got away.

She drove slowly down the road, her window open, breathing in the sweet scent of crab apples. She kept to the old familiar routes, heading out west as far as Tubby's Lake, then circling back toward town. She drove past Grace's street, but didn't turn in. Every landmark she passed seemed to lurch up at her, dragging her back. She drove on, determined. Everything caught her eye.

VIDALIA ONION a new sign announced, paint still wet. It was propped against the front wheel of a car backed up to the railroad tracks on the dead side of the depot. A man and his children were busy, were happy, arranging cabbages on the fenders. There were trays of tomatoes and (she craned to be sure) the year's first peaches. A baby sat in the driver's seat tooting the horn. As Angelina went by, the baby leaned from the window and waved a tattered little rebel flag.

At the next corner Angelina stopped (YIELD TO PEDESTRIANS was painted man-sized in the road both ways) to let Mrs. Nesby in her fresh print dress cross the street on her way to the library to return a Janice Holt Giles. She blew Angelina a God-bless-you kiss. A quarter of a mile farther north the Highway Department was surveying. The yellow Travelall was parked with its door open, and a flagman was stopping traffic in both directions.

"Left . . . left . . . left . . . right . . . WHOA! Whoa!"

Tap-tap-tap. They were using an ax for a hammer to drive the pins in. It was warm enough for the chain-pullers and target men to go shirtless. Their visibility vests were stark against their winter-pale skin. Each man (there were six, Angelina noticed: six strong men, like pallbearers) had hold of the tape or chain or stick or rod. The ledger man stared through the transit and shouted, "Left . . . left . . . left . . . good . . . WHOA!" and then again, the tap-tap-tap.

The flagman noticed Angelina checking her watch. "Won't be long now," he estimated. The crew was already snaking its way down the street toward the next mark. Then the flagman swung his STOP sign out of service to SLOW and waved her past. "Sorry for the delay," he called.

Angelina drove north till she came to the scar where the new road was being graded. She turned down the diminishing old farm track toward the reservoir and rode till the young weeds and brambles scratched and clawed her to a stop. She could feel the earth rumbling from the prime movers a mile away chewing up the red hills into four lanes. She set the brake and rolled up the window against the dust. She left her pocketbook and keys. She took only the little pistol.

She had not been here before. She looked around her for a place. There were birdfoot violets in the dry clay. She had always loved them, yet none she had ever transplanted survived to bloom the next year. She bent to pick one, then changed her mind. A C-130 on a training flight made a slow turn and headed out over the lake toward the mountains. She watched it till it was only a noise on the horizon, then she sought out the tender-green shade beneath a broken willow. She aimed the gun approximately at her heart and pulled the trigger.

The noise as much as the charge toppled her. She thought, I should have been lying down! Too late. She had planned to cease instantly, and this delay caused her chagrin; she failed, as she had all her life, by degrees. She stared up into the ferny, fretted crown of the willow. "Oh, soon, oh soon oh soon," she panted, laboring to deliver herself of this final burden, life. She lay watching the sky go white as a shell over her. All the color bled from the day. A jay spotted her, flew over to investigate, hopped lower in the branches, and cried THIEF! THIEF! as he flew away west to shrill the news. Soon that sound was lost in the surf-roar of her inner ear, and Angelina lost contact . . .

No one had the least notion. They called around when she failed to show up at the Tupperware party, and Grace finally called Chick at work. But he didn't begin worrying until Bonnie called too; she was due at the orthodontist's and Angelina had not come by school to pick her up as she had promised. Chick guessed then it was car trouble. No one guessed it would turn out as it did.

The reservoir manager noticed her car on toward sundown, went to check on it, and found her, so she didn't have to lie out there all night.

She was in surgery till nearly midnight, and in the waiting room the little crowd of shocked well-wishers gradually thinned to Angelina's husband, her father, her daughter, and a few silent comforters. Bonnie, from the first, felt indicted, never mind who pulled the trigger. She was her mother's child all right, and the tenderest victim. She kept to herself, and spent hours in the rest room; Chick could hear her congested crying but didn't know how to help her. He couldn't even help himself. When the surgeon came out and told them Angelina would live, Bonnie had her mama's note, tear-stained now and folded, folded into triviality, as though it were some everyday something that could be forgotten, left behind in an ashtray, lost in a pocket, unimportant. (All the note said was *Job 7*— that's all she wrote, addressed *To Whom It May Concern*, not to Chick and Bonnie, not even *Sorry*, not even *Love*, as though in forgetting everything she lived for she forgot them first. Bonnie had looked up the quote in the little white calf-bound King James Angelina had given her for Christmas. She read and reread that whole early chapter from "Is there not an appointed time?" to the last exulting despair of "For now I shall sleep in the dust; and thou shalt seek me in the morning but I shall not be.") Bonnie, in a wizened whisper in the general echoing ignorance, asked the surgeon, asked anyone, "Why?" She turned on them all, on herself in the dark glass of the midnight windows and shouted it this time, "Why didn't she want to read to the end of the book?"

Which is, of course, the question. Her father, her grandfather, Reverend Martin, Dr. Spence, the neighbors—all met her harrowing, wild gaze for a moment only, then looked away.

In the morning they let Chick go in and see her for five minutes. Angelina was awake, but she lay with her eyes shut against him, her chin aimed at God. She knew as well as if she were floating in a corner of the ceiling looking down at him exactly what Chick was doing, heard him lift the one chair and turn it around and straddle it and sit, knew he was resting his chin on his fists, watching her. Four of his minutes, then thirty seconds more, elapsed. Finally she had to open her eyes and let him in.

"Oh, babe," he said when she looked his way. "You very nearly broke my heart."

She beat at the bed with her pale hands, clawing at

the IV's in her wrists that tethered her to life. The nurse came, then another, and they restrained her. Chick turned at the door for a last look.

Septic with regret, he didn't have time to arrange his face before Bonnie saw him. Terrified, she cried, "She didn't die, did she? She'll have another chance?"

He thought of Angelina lying there small and sharp-eyed and at bay somehow, vulnerable but valiant, like a little beast who would gnaw off its own foot to escape the trap.

"Another chance," he said.